ChangelingPress.com

March (Underland MC 3)
A Bad Boys MC Romance
Harley Wylde

March (Underland MC 3)
A Bad Boys MC Romance
Harley Wylde

All rights reserved.
Copyright ©2025

ISBN: 978-1-60521-938-7

Publisher:
Changeling Press LLC
315 N. Centre St.
Martinsburg, WV 25404
ChangelingPress.com

Printed in the U.S.A.

Editor: Crystal Esau
Cover Artist: Bryan Keller

The individual stories in this anthology have been previously released in E-Book format.

No part of this publication may be reproduced or shared by any electronic or mechanical means, including but not limited to reprinting, photocopying, or digital reproduction, without prior written permission from Changeling Press LLC.

This book contains sexually explicit scenes and adult language which some may find offensive and which is not appropriate for a young audience. Changeling Press books are for sale to adults, only, as defined by the laws of the country in which you made your purchase.

Table of Contents

March (Underland MC 3) 4
Chapter One 5
Chapter Two 14
Chapter Three 24
Chapter Four 32
Chapter Five 40
Chapter Six 50
Chapter Seven 60
Chapter Eight 71
Chapter Nine 80
Chapter Ten 88
Chapter Eleven 96
Chapter Twelve 105
Chapter Thirteen 114
Chapter Fourteen 124
Chapter Fifteen 133
Chapter Sixteen 144
Chapter Seventeen 153
Chapter Eighteen 161
Chapter Nineteen 169
Epilogue 178
Harley Wylde 184
Bad Boys Multiverse 185
Changeling Press LLC 186

March (Underland MC 3)
A Bad Boys MC Romance
Harley Wylde

Sometimes the most forbidden love can be the most irresistible...

Violet -- My brother gave his life for his country, and without him, I lived in pure hell. My family was the type you read about in horror stories. When I went away to college, I thought everything would be better... Until a frat party went horribly wrong. Now I'm pregnant, lost, and so very alone. So I did the one thing I told myself I'd never do. I used my computer skills in a not very legal way to look up my brother's best friend -- Marcus Blevins. Once he lets me in, I know I'll do anything to stay.

March -- I joined the military, and even after I my friend and brother-in-arms lost his life. There's no going back after that. How could I ever face his little sister, Violet? I never thought she'd track me down -- or that she could -- but when she showed up on the clubhouse doorstep, I can't look the other way. I'll make them all pay for what they did. The more time I spend with Violet, the more I fall under her spell. If her brother knew the sorts of thoughts I'm having, he'd come back from the dead to kick my ass. But just maybe I need Vi as much as she needs me.

Suspense, passion, and second chances -- are you ready to dive into this captivating tale?

Chapter One
March

The smell of gunpowder lingered in the air, a ghostly reminder that clung to my nostrils even now. I sat on the edge of my bed in the dimly lit room, the shadows casting long fingers across the floor like they were reaching for me. My mind was a battlefield, a relentless onslaught of memories storming the barricades I'd painstakingly built.

Ben's face flashed before my eyes -- laughter silenced by the crack of a distant sniper's bullet. The way his body crumpled, as if strings had been cut from a marionette. Blood staining the earth beneath him, dark and spreading like a sinister shadow. The sound of gunfire echoed in my ears, a cacophony of death that never seemed to fade. It was all so vivid, too real, as if time hadn't moved forward since that fateful day.

I clenched my fists, the knuckles turning white as bone. The pain of the memory was a physical thing, a vise tightening around my chest. I gritted my teeth, each breath a struggle against the tide of grief that threatened to pull me under.

"Focus," I muttered to myself. I couldn't let the past consume me -- not when my brothers needed me alert and ready. We hadn't finished cleaning up the town of Warren yet. Until the mayor and his assistant were out of the picture, anything could happen.

But in my mind, I still saw Ben's lifeless eyes staring back at me, an unspoken accusation. Why him? Why not me? I'd asked myself that question too many times to count. The guilt was a relentless enemy, gnawing away at the edges of my sanity.

"Damnit!" The curse was wrenched from somewhere deep within, a primal sound of frustration and rage. I stood abruptly, knocking a picture off my nightstand. The glass shattered on impact, the sound filling the silence like a gunshot.

"Keep it together, Blevins." My voice was a low growl, the words meant to steel my resolve. But there was no escaping the war inside my head. It was a constant companion, a familiar foe that knew all my defenses. I went into the bathroom, splashing water on my face, hoping the crisp coolness would snap my mind out of the nightmare plaguing me even when I was awake.

"Can't let them see you break," I reminded myself, staring at the stranger in the mirror, a man with haunted eyes. A soldier. A biker. A brother. All woven into one man who couldn't afford the luxury of breaking down.

"*Semper Fi*," I whispered, invoking the oath that still bound me, even in this new battlefield. Always faithful, even when faith was hard to come by. I had to be strong. There was no other choice. For the club. For myself. For Ben.

The silence of my room was a siren call, urging me to dwell in the darkness of my thoughts. But I couldn't. I wouldn't. With a last look at the space that held too much sorrow, I turned away from the ghosts that sought to claim me.

Laughter snuck through the walls, a jarring symphony of life that felt worlds away. I paused, my hand hovering over the doorknob. The echo of camaraderie was a beacon, yet it stirred an unease in my gut -- a battle between isolation's allure and the pull of brotherhood.

"Come on, March," I muttered to myself, my fingers wrapping around the cold metal. "You can't hide forever."

Tonight, I would face the living, not the dead.

My boots thudded against the floor. I could feel the hum of the clubhouse growing louder, the voices melding into one another, forming a tapestry of comfort and familiarity that I both longed for and resented.

I entered the main room and saw most of my brothers were present. Mock and Knave were both gone, most likely out looking for women. I didn't see Jo or Eliza, even though their men were here. I wondered if they were working on their book, or just enjoying some alone time.

Cheshire's grin flickered with the mischief of a man who knew too much. Or maybe he'd seen too much and had lost a good bit of his sanity like the rest of us.

"March." Hatter nodded. "Take a seat and join us."

"Long day?" Cheshire asked, but his eyes held a depth of understanding.

"Something like that," I replied.

The atmosphere was thick with the scent of spilled beer and the buzz of stories being traded back and forth. It was a living entity this place, a sanctuary built on the unspoken bonds of men who'd seen the darkest corners of the world and lived to tell the tale.

I took a seat, the chair scraping against the worn floorboards. Here, amidst the laughter and the clinking of bottles, I found a momentary reprieve from the ghost haunting me.

"Drink?" Hatter offered, sliding a bottle toward me. I noticed there were a few unopened beers, and the table next to us had more than a dozen empties.

"Thanks." The glass was cool against my palm, a small anchor to the present.

Around us, the clubhouse thrived, a hive of activity and life that seemed almost defiant in its vibrancy. These men, these brothers, they were survivors. We all were.

"Here's to living." Cheshire raised his bottle, and Hatter followed suit.

"Here's to living," I echoed, and for a fleeting second, the weight inside lifted. It wouldn't last. It never did, but I'd take the reprieve while I could.

The clink of my bottle against theirs sounded like a starting pistol. For a brief moment, it transported me to another time and place. But as soon as I blinked, I was back in the present.

"Remember that time in Kandahar?" Hatter asked. "When March here decided to play chicken with an incoming convoy?"

"Playing chicken?" Cheshire's grin was all teeth. "More like he had a death wish."

"Didn't have a wish for dying," I grunted. "Had a plan for living."

"Damn straight," Hatter said. "You led them right into the ambush."

"Saved our asses," Cheshire chimed in, lifting his bottle in a silent salute.

"Ben would've done the same," I muttered, and then the chatter around us faded.

"March..." Hatter's eyes met mine, steady as ever.

"Ben was... he was..." My throat tightened around the words. Hatter and Cheshire may have known him, but not like I did. We'd been best friends since we were kids. Losing him had felt like I'd lost a family member.

"Best of us," Cheshire finished for me, his usual smirk wiped clean.

"Never got to tell him… just how much…" The words were stilted and hard to get out.

"March, Ben knew," Hatter stated, firm and resolute. "He knew."

"Knew what?" I asked, even though I feared the answer.

"That we're brothers. All of us," Hatter replied. I knew what he meant. Sometimes family went beyond blood.

"Brothers 'til the end," Cheshire echoed quietly, and we drank to that unspoken truth.

The silence lingered like a thick fog, heavy enough to choke on. Cheshire broke it first, his voice uncharacteristically gentle. "We've all got ghosts, brother. Some just scream louder than others. You and Ben… Well, you had a longer history than the rest of us had with him. And you were right there when it happened."

No shit. Some nights, I still felt the spray of his blood coating my skin. The warmth of it searing me like hot coals.

"Damn right," Hatter added. "Lost too many to count. Each one leaves a mark, but you keep going. Because that's what warriors do."

My fists unclenched slowly, the white of my knuckles fading back to flesh. Their words, raw and honest, chiseled away at the walls I'd built.

"Remember Rico?" Cheshire asked, tipping his chair back, his blue eyes clouding over. "Took three bullets meant for me. I hear his laugh sometimes, in the wind. It's like he's still here, riding with us."

"Rico was a good man." Hatter nodded solemnly. "Died a warrior's death."

"And Ben… he died a hero's death," I murmured, finally finding the strength to lift my gaze.

"Heroes, every last one," Hatter agreed. His piercing eyes held mine, not letting me sink back into the dark. "And we carry them with us, every mile of the road."

"Every damn mile," I echoed, feeling the truth in his words weave through the pain.

"Look around, March," Cheshire said, gesturing to the crowded room. "This is family. We're your brothers, through thick and thin. We may not have all made it out of there alive, but our fallen brothers will live on in our memories. As long as we remember them, they'll never truly die."

I scanned the clubhouse, the familiar scents of oil and leather wrapping around me like a balm. Laughter bounced off the walls, and the warmth soaked into me. This place, these men, they were my sanctuary in a world laced with chaos.

"Family," I whispered, allowing the word to settle in my chest.

"Always," Hatter affirmed, reaching across the table to clasp my shoulder.

"Let's drink to that," Cheshire said, an edge of his grin returning. He raised his beer, and Hatter and I followed suit, our bottles clinking.

The tension drained from my body, seeping into the floorboards below. In its place, something warm unfurled, a sense of peace I hadn't felt in a long time. It never lasted. Wouldn't. Couldn't. I took what little bits of solace I could find here and there. It was the only way to remain even somewhat sane.

"Brothers," I said, meeting their eyes. The bond between us, forged in blood and fire, was unbreakable.

"Until the end," they replied in unison.

For the first time in what felt like forever, laughter bubbled up from deep within me, genuine and freeing. I was home, surrounded by my brothers, and for now, that was all I needed. And when the nightmares returned, I'd have to remind myself of this moment, and all the ones like it we'd shared since we became civilians again.

The room hushed as I stood, beer in hand, eyes scanning the faces of my brothers. Each one carried scars, tales etched in flesh and soul. The air was thick with unspoken understanding, an electric current of shared loss that hummed beneath our skin. I knew they could tell by the look in my eyes that I'd been fighting my demons before I came in here. Each man had done the same, countless times.

"Tonight," I started, "we remember those who aren't here to raise a glass. Ben. Rico. Tate." My throat tightened, a noose of grief tugging with every name.

"Vick," Rabbit said, lifting his beer.

"Jarret," Tweedle said.

"To our fallen brothers, may the road they ride be smooth and endless," I said.

"Ride free," the chorus echoed back, a haunting melody of respect and remembrance.

I drank, the bitter brew sliding down my throat. Swallowed past the lump that never quite faded. With each sip, a silent oath to never forget.

I lowered my bottle, the weight of brotherhood heavy in my chest. A patchwork family bound tighter than blood could ever dictate. It gave purpose to the pain, a beacon in the tempest that was my mind.

They didn't know how much they kept me anchored, these men who shared my demons. How the roar of engines and their gruff voices were the only lullabies capable of quieting the cacophony of war that still played on a loop in my head.

"March." Hatter's voice cut through my

reflection. "They'd be damn proud of you."

"Damn right," Cheshire added, his smirk betraying the moisture in his eyes.

Pride mingled with the sorrow, a bittersweet cocktail that warmed from within. This club, this duty I bore, it was more than a title or a role. It was a lifeline -- a reason to keep pushing when darkness clawed at my edges.

"Thanks," I managed, my voice raw. "Couldn't do it without you bastards."

Laughter erupted, a salve to the open wounds. In their company, even the deepest cuts seemed to heal, if just for a moment.

Once a Marine, always a Marine. But here, in the Underland MC, we were more. We were guardians of each other's sanity, keepers of stories too grim for the light of day. And protectors of this town.

I looked around at my brothers, their faces as hard as the lives we led, yet there was warmth there too. They were the pillars in the chaos, the constant in a life that had offered little else.

In the safety of shadows, where the world couldn't reach us, we were invincible. And in that moment, I allowed myself to believe it. We'd already battled several times in this place we now called home, and we'd been lucky enough to not lose anyone.

Outside these walls, danger prowled, hungry and relentless. It clawed at the edges of our sanctuary, waiting for a crack to slip through, a weakness to exploit.

"Tomorrow's ride is going to be dicey," I said. "But we ride together, through whatever shitstorm comes our way."

More than once, the damn mayor had done his best to ambush us. I'd hoped after we got rid of the sheriff, things would be different. The mayor had seemed like an easy target in comparison, but I'd been wrong. We'd been at odds with him for months now, and the bastard was still in office. But not for much longer. I refused to let him be.

The night deepened, wrapping the clubhouse in its dark embrace. We stood at the precipice, the future uncertain, but together we faced the abyss.

Laughter and conversation carried us late into the night, a brief respite before dawn would bring new challenges. But for now, I belonged -- one part of an unbreakable chain.

Chapter Two
March

I was mid-way through a stack of reports when the knock came. Three sharp raps, insistent and out of place against the background hum of classic rock and the occasional clink of beer bottles. I stood, leaving the papers sprawled carelessly, and made my way to the door.

The clubhouse was my domain. I was the gatekeeper here, Sergeant-at-Arms of Underland MC, and unannounced visitors were rare. The knock echoed again, more urgent this time, pulling me faster toward the heavy oak barrier.

I yanked it open. Blinking, I wondered if I was hallucinating. "Vi?"

Violet Benson. A ghost from a past life stood on the weathered porch, drenched in shadows. Didn't matter I hadn't seen her in a long ass time, I'd recognize her anywhere. Her whiskey eyes were wide, brimming with fear, her long dark hair a tangled veil across one side of her face. She looked small, fragile against the night's chill, but her presence hit me like a freight train.

"Marcus..." Her voice cracked, a mere whisper carried by the wind.

What the hell was she doing here? Years had passed since I'd seen her -- since Ben... No. I shoved that thought back into its dark corner. My gaze swept over her, taking in the trembling hands and the desperate plea etched into every line of her body.

"Vi?" I repeated, my voice betraying none of the turmoil that churned inside. "What are you running from? And how the hell are you here?"

She hesitated, lip caught between her teeth, and

something protective flared within me, despite my better judgment. This was Violet, Ben's little sister, not just some stray looking for shelter.

"Can I come in?" The question hung in the air.

I studied her a moment longer, the discipline of my military days screaming at me to maintain the perimeter, to keep the unknown at bay. Yet there she stood, a living reminder of promises unkept, and debts unpaid.

"Marcus, please…"

"It's March. I don't go by Marcus here." I stepped aside, breaking protocol with the weight of her gaze. The door creaked on its hinges as I let her pass, the scent of rain clinging to her. The clubhouse would never be the same after tonight, and neither would we.

"March, I'm in trouble." Violet's voice cracked as she stepped into the dim light of the clubhouse. Her gaze darted around before settling back on me. "I didn't know where else to go."

I closed the door behind her, shutting out the night and any prying eyes. I'd never told her where I was going. Not once had I contacted anyone back home. The fact she was standing here made my senses scream. Something wasn't right.

"Talk to me, Vi." My words were a command.

Her breath hitched, and she clutched at her stomach, a motion unmistakable in its meaning. "I'm pregnant, March." The bomb dropped, and the reverberations shook the very foundation of my resolve.

"Jesus, Violet…" I ran a hand over my face, my mind reeling. Pregnant. Vulnerable. And here, in my world -- a world that had no place for innocence. I was far too fucked up. The simple fact Hatter was expecting a kid made me nervous. But now Vi…

"I can't do this alone." Her plea sliced through my defenses, leaving me exposed to memories I fought hard to bury.

Ben's laugh echoed in my skull, a sound that used to mean safety, now twisted into a taunt from the grave. I couldn't save him. Maybe Vi was here to give me a second chance, the opportunity to make things right. I couldn't bring her brother back, but I could ensure her safety.

"Who's after you?" I asked, needing facts, something concrete to hold onto amidst the flood of guilt.

"Doesn't matter," she whispered. "They'll find me."

"Like hell they will." The words left my lips before I could rein them in, the protective instinct taking command -- the same one that failed Ben when he needed it most.

My gut churned with the turmoil of decisions stacked like dominoes. Help her, and I'd drag the club into whatever mess she was tangled up in. Turn her away, and I'd be abandoning the last piece of a man who had been more than a brother to me.

"March, please..." There it was again, that tremor in her voice, pulling at me.

"All right." I locked my jaw, my decision made despite the screaming protests of caution. "You're under our protection now."

"Thank --"

"Don't thank me yet." I cut her off, my gaze locking onto hers. "This is not charity, Vi. It's a debt being repaid."

She gave a brisk nod, no longer holding my gaze.

"Come on," I grunted, leading her to a table. Heads turned. Conversations stalled. The Underland

MC's pulse slowed, every eye now fixed on the girl who'd brought trouble to our doorstep.

"Boys," I announced, my voice low, "this is Violet."

"Violet?" Hatter's brow creased as he stood, his height commanding attention. His voice, though quiet, never failed to fill the room. "The name's familiar."

"Ben's sister," I said, the words tasting like ash.

"Ah." Hatter's eyes narrowed, taking in Violet's skittish stance. "And what brings Ben's shadow here?"

"Refuge," I replied, before she could. Her secrets weren't mine to spill, not yet. Hell, I still didn't even know them, other than the one in her belly.

Cheshire leaned back in his chair, that ever-present grin flickering at the edges of his lips. "Refuge. From what kind of storm, I wonder?"

"Doesn't matter." I met Cheshire's gaze, hard as flint. "She's under our protection now."

"Is she?" Absolem chimed in, his voice rough as gravel. He sized Violet up, skepticism etched into the lines of his face.

"March has spoken," Hatter declared, his word final. But the question remained, dancing in their eyes, unvoiced but loud as thunder -- why? "But it also means she's his responsibility."

Violet stayed close, her breaths shallow. She watched them, her eyes wavering with uncertainty, but beneath it all, there was something else. A spark of steel, forged in fires I hadn't witnessed. She'd survive, this one. I wondered what she'd been through, and if I'd been to blame for any of it. I should have kept in touch, made sure she was all right. It's what Ben would have wanted.

The clubhouse settled into a low hum, the brothers dispersing with wary glances thrown over their shoulders.

"Violet," I began, my voice steady despite the storm I sensed brewing within her. "Tell me everything."

She hugged herself. The silence stretched, and I started to think she'd never speak.

"They... he..." Her voice cracked, failing her.

"Take your time." My stance softened, but my senses remained alert. Every instinct screamed at me to shield her from whatever hunted her outside these walls.

"Raped." The word fell like a stone into the quiet. "That's how -- how I got pregnant."

My jaw clenched so tight I thought it might shatter. Rage swirled, a tempest held at bay by sheer will. "Who?"

"Doesn't matter," she whispered, a tear tracing a path down her cheek. "He's gone now. Dead."

"Good." One less monster to hunt. But that didn't ease the weight pressing on my chest.

"March..." Violet's eyes met mine, stark with fear. "I'm scared. All the time. What if --"

"Stop." I cut her off, stepping closer. "No one will touch you here. Underland is your fortress now."

"Thank you," she breathed, a shudder passing through her.

"Who knows about the baby?"

"Nobody. Just you." She wrapped her arms around her stomach, protective. "I ran before they could find out."

"Who's 'they'?" The Sergeant-at-Arms in me demanded details. Risks needed assessing, threats needed to be neutralized. Not to mention she'd said the person responsible was dead. Now it was a *they*.

"Old ghosts." Her voice dropped to a haunted

whisper. "It's complicated."

"Complicated's our middle name." I crossed my arms, my gaze never wavering from hers. "We'll sort it."

"March, I --" She choked back a sob. "I can't drag you into this mess."

"Too late for that, Vi." I stepped into her space, my tone resolute. "You're under our roof. Your mess is my mess now. Should have known that before you showed up here."

"Thank you," she repeated, her body sagging with relief I knew was far from complete.

"I'll show you to a room. Get some rest," I instructed. "Tomorrow we'll plan your next move. We keep you safe. We keep the kid safe."

"Okay." She nodded, the steel in her returning.

I walked her to an empty room, the one Eliza had used before she paired off with Cheshire. Hell, if we kept taking in women, we were going to need more space. I pushed open the door, flicked on the light, and ushered her inside.

"Bedding is clean. Towels are under the sink in the bathroom." I pointed to the open door to the right. "Goodnight, Violet."

I watched her retreat into the room and shut the door.

"Goodnight, March." Her voice, barely above a whisper, carried a note of something new. Trust, maybe. Or hope. Just the same, I heard her through the closed door.

"Goodnight" was a promise. And I intended to keep it. Whatever chased after her, I'd make sure it couldn't harm her within these walls.

I stood watch in the hall long after she disappeared into the guest room. Even though I should have gone to my own room, or back to my reports, I couldn't make myself leave her yet. I couldn't shake it -- Violet's fear had sunk its claws into me, pulling at threads I thought I'd cut loose years ago.

I heard a door open behind me. My senses were on high alert and I heard the soft tread of footsteps. Vi's.

"March?" Her voice was timid but cut through the silence like a knife.

"Right here, Vi." I didn't turn. "You should be resting."

"I can't," she murmured. "Every time I close my eyes --"

"Hey." I spun around, ready to face whatever demons chased her from sleep. Her eyes glinted with unshed tears in the dim light. I stepped closer, fighting back the urge to shield her from the world with my own body. "Talk to me."

Her breath hitched. "I'm scared, March. All the time. I don't know if I can do this alone."

"You're not alone. Not anymore."

Violet nodded, biting down on her pouty lip. The sight sent a jolt through me. "How can you be so sure?"

"Because." I paused, choosing my next words carefully. "Because I've seen war, Vi. I've seen what people can survive. And there's a fire in you, something fierce. You're going to make it through this, and I'll be right here."

"Even after all this time?" Her voice was small, but her gaze never wavered.

"Especially after all this time." I let the truth of it sink into my bones. "I owe Ben that much."

"Ben…" She whispered his name like a benediction, and I knew then that I'd step into hell itself before I let anything touch her again. I'd failed him by letting her get hurt. Never again.

"Let's get through tonight," I said. "We'll figure out the rest come morning."

"Okay." She exhaled slowly, visibly trying to steady herself. "Thank you, March."

"Nothing to thank me for." I offered her a tight smile, the kind that didn't quite reach my eyes.

For a moment, her lips curled into a semblance of a smile. It was faint, but it was there -- a hint of the resilience that clung to her.

"Get some sleep, Violet." I wanted to say more, to ease the crease that worry had etched into her brow, but words seemed suddenly inadequate.

"Stay with me?" The question hung between us.

"I'll be right here."

She hesitated, and I wondered if she needed something more from me. Instead, she nodded and backed up a step.

"Goodnight," she finally said, her tone carrying the weight of unsaid things.

I watched her walk back to her temporary sanctuary, feeling the shift between us. The door shut with a click, and I stood there in the dim hallway, my thoughts tumultuous. The way Violet's eyes had darted around earlier, scanning shadows like they were alive, told me we were stepping into a maelstrom neither of us might be ready for. My gut knotted up -- the same pre-battle twist I remembered from my days overseas. Only this time, there was a baby's life on the line.

"March?" Her voice drifted out, muffled by walls but clear in its uncertainty.

"Still here," I called back.

The clubhouse was quiet now, the raucous

laughter long faded into the night. But danger never really slept. It waited, patient as a viper. This world didn't take kindly to vulnerability. It chewed up the scared and the weak, spit them out without a second thought. And Violet, with her whiskey eyes and steel spine, she was anything but weak -- but she was carrying something precious, something that made her a target.

I could almost hear the clock ticking, each second pulling us deeper into a future rife with threat. But men who could hurt a woman that way were monsters, which meant we had something they didn't -- whoever *they* may be -- brotherhood, loyalty, a bond forged in fire and blood. The Underland MC wasn't just a club. It was a fortress against the chaos. And I was the damned gatekeeper.

"Are we safe here?" she called out through the closed door.

"Violet, listen to me." I stepped closer, pressing my palm against the cool wood, needing the connection. "You're under our protection now. Under my protection. I'm not letting anyone hurt you."

"Your word is solid?"

"Yes," I affirmed, and it wasn't just talk.

"Thank you," she whispered. "March?"

"Yeah?"

"Thank you," she said again. "For everything."

"Save it for when we're out of the woods, Vi. For now, rest. I mean it. Sleep this time."

"Okay."

As she hopefully drifted to sleep on the other side of the door, my mind was already waging war on the unseen enemies lurking in the shadows. We were in for a hell of a fight -- a fight for her safety, for the life growing inside her, for a peace that seemed as elusive as smoke. But I'd walk through fire before I let anything happen to Violet or her kid. She was family now, whether she knew it or not.

Chapter Three
Violet

The morning light crept in, pale and intrusive. I blinked against it, my heart quickening as unfamiliar surroundings came into focus. The sheets felt too crisp, the air too still. For a split second, panic clawed up my throat -- then it all flooded back. Underland MC. March. Safety.

I exhaled slowly, pushing the blankets off with a shiver. The floor was cold beneath my bare feet. This wasn't just any haven. I had a feeling it was going to be so much more. A stronghold. Not the building itself. No, what made it safe was March.

Standing up took effort. My muscles were tight, coiled with the tension of the last few days. Or had it been weeks? Time blurred when running on fear.

In the attached bathroom, I faced my reflection. The girl staring back at me had whiskey-colored eyes too large for her face, dark hair tangled from restless sleep. She looked like she'd seen hell. Maybe she had.

"Keep moving, Vi," I murmured.

The faucet's metallic scent filled the small space as I washed up. Cold water splashed over my skin, grounding me, washing away the remnants of nightmares that clung like cobwebs. I patted my face dry with a towel. I even found a new toothbrush and small tube of toothpaste. Assuming they were okay to use, I quickly brushed my teeth and rinsed my mouth.

March. I needed to find him. He was the anchor in this storm, the promise of protection I hadn't known I'd craved until I landed in this mess.

I left the bathroom, my steps hesitant but determined. The common room would be busy now, the club members starting their day. Or so I assumed. I didn't know them yet, really, but I had to navigate this new world somehow. For my child. For me.

It was time to stop running, time to start fighting. With a deep breath, I stepped into the common room, scanning the space for the man who'd promised to help me rewrite my future.

My heart thrummed. Eyes slid over me, quick and assessing. I clutched the fabric of my shirt, felt it dampen under my grip.

March was there, his back to the wall, eyes like chips of ice cutting across the room to meet mine. A path cleared as I moved, toward him. The two women at the bar, their laughter a jarring note in the tense air, caught my attention. They looked tough, unbreakable -- so different from the fragile thing I felt inside.

"Violet," March's voice rumbled, low and commanding. Every muscle in my body tensed, then relaxed. His presence alone did that -- calmed the chaos.

I picked up the pace, closing the distance between us until I stood before him, acutely aware of the space he occupied. With a crooked finger, he beckoned. Closer, closer. My steps quickened I was so eager for the safety he promised without words.

"Sit," he said, almost gentle. The chair scraped the floor, an abrasive sound that matched the rawness in my throat. I sank into it.

March's gaze never wavered, piercing through the last remnants of my fear, anchoring me to the here and now. March's glare sliced through the buzz of conversation. One by one, the others shuffled out, leaving nothing but silence behind. The two women at the bar cast me a look I couldn't read before following suit.

"Talk to me, Vi," March said, voice low and

steady as bedrock. "I need to know what you've been through. I didn't get much from you last night, but I need to know it all."

The words jostled in my chest, each one a shard of glass scraping its way up my throat. My hands trembled on my lap.

"Back home..." My voice was a whisper, fractured and faint. "There were always guys who didn't know how to take 'no' for an answer. I'd managed to avoid them, until..."

"When you say they wouldn't take no for an answer... Did they hurt you?" March's question came with a dangerous edge, his blue eyes darkening like storm clouds. It was clear he already knew the answer, but for some reason needed me to spell it out for him.

I nodded, a solitary tear betraying the dam I'd built. "It wasn't just him. There were others. Memories are... they're foggy. But I remember enough."

"When you say enough, it's obvious you're scared if you came all the way here, but how much do you remember?"

"Not exactly everything. But what I do remember leaves me feeling terrified." The word hung heavy between us, a specter of my past. "Every touch is a reminder. Every glance feels like judgment. It all comes to me in flickers. Bits and pieces. But it's enough to know what they did."

March leaned forward, elbows on knees, bridging the gap. "You're not alone anymore, Vi. We stand together here. Tell me what you need."

"Justice," I breathed. "Safety for my child."

"Then that's what you'll get."

The room felt too big, the silence too loud. March's gaze never wavered from my face, his eyes searching for the pieces of a puzzle only I could complete.

"Vi," he said, his voice softer now, "whatever you can remember might help us find them."

I swallowed hard, willing my heartbeat to slow. "It was late. The bar had just closed. I'd been working there since I was eighteen. Waiting tables, even though I wasn't supposed to touch the liquor." Each word scraped against my raw insides. "I thought I was alone."

"Did you know him?" His words were precise, cutting through the haze of my memories.

"His face... it's blurry. But his voice..." A shiver raced down my spine. "It was deep, mocking."

"Anything else? A tattoo, a ring, something unique?"

"Scars," I muttered, the image surfacing like an apparition in my mind. "On his knuckles. Like he'd been in fights." My voice steadied with the detail.

"Good." March's nod was approval, encouragement. "We'll start there."

"Will we find him? It's not much to go on. His hair was... dark, I think."

March's expression hardened, the promise in his eyes as sharp as a blade. "We don't stop until we do."

The memory surged forward, a relentless tide. "He pushed me against the wall," I said, my voice steadier than I felt. My fingers curled into fists on my lap, nails digging into my palms. The fear was still there, icy and suffocating, but beneath it, something else simmered. A fierce resolve. "I fought. I scratched his face." I could almost feel the ghost of his skin under my nails.

"Keep going." March's approval was a lifeline.

The room blurred, but I blinked it back into focus. I told him about the sensation of hands tearing at my clothes. The way I was held down as they took turns using me.

"Last night you said the baby's father was dead. Were you pregnant before that happened?" he asked.

I shook my head. I'd lied to him, not wanting to explain things last night. I'd been too exhausted.

"So he's one of the men who raped you?"

"Yes," I said. "I hadn't been with anyone else in months. Afterward, I was too scared to tell the police. I wasn't supposed to be working at the bar. Got treated by a woman in the neighborhood. Later, when I was throwing up my breakfast, I went to the clinic. They not only ran a pregnancy test but checks for STDs too. I'm clean, in case you were wondering. Thankfully, all they gave me were nightmares and a baby."

March leaned in, his blue eyes scanning my face. "How did you find me?"

"I..." A twinge of pride nudged at the shame as I met his gaze. "I hacked into multiple government offices and followed the paper trail."

"You what?" His eyebrows shot up, a rare crack in his stoic facade.

"Turns out college wasn't a total waste." I managed a half-smile, even as my heart hammered against my ribs. "I've got skills, March."

"Clearly." He leaned back, regarding me with newfound respect. "Hacking, huh?"

"Desperation makes you resourceful." The words hung heavy in the air, a testament to the lengths I'd go to protect my future.

March's nod was slow, deliberate. "Never underestimate a mother," he murmured, more to himself than to me.

"Or someone with nothing left to lose."

His jaw tightened, the set of his mouth telling me

he understood all too well. In that moment, I knew March would become an ally. March's gaze never wavered from mine, a silent acknowledgment of the admission I'd just made.

"You've got a set of skills we could use," he said, his voice low but carrying across the stillness that had settled between us. "There's rot at the city's core. Corruption we've been trying to expose. You in?"

I felt the weight of his question -- an offer to be part of something larger than myself. It was a chance to take back control, to fight against the darkness instead of being consumed by it.

"Okay," I replied, my response more a breath than a word, but it was enough.

"Good." He stood up, the movement fluid, like a predator uncoiling. "Let's get you introduced. Properly this time."

March led me into a kitchen with a large table. Big enough for everyone to fit around it, and still leave room for more.

"Listen up!" March's voice cut through the hum of conversation, commanding attention. "As I said last night, this is Violet and she's Ben's sister. It turns out she has some talent we can use. Actually, Absolem, she may have you beat when it comes to a computer."

The members of the Underland MC looked at me, not with pity, but with something akin to respect. No words were exchanged, but the nods and subtle shifts in posture told me all I needed to know. I was under their wing now, and in their silent acceptance, I found an unexpected sense of security.

"Violet," a voice called out. I turned to see a woman waving at me. "We're glad you're here. I'm Jo. Let me know if you need anything."

"Thanks." I wasn't sure where she fit into this

crew.

"I'm Eliza," said the woman beside her. "I'm with Cheshire. Jo is with Hatter."

Jo's eyebrow arched. "And you're with March?"

My cheeks flushed. Only in my dreams.

"Stop playing matchmaker," March said.

"Take a seat, get comfortable. We look after our own here," Eliza said, gesturing to the chair beside her.

I sat, surrounded by the strength of these women. They didn't know my full story yet, but their acceptance didn't require it.

After a while, March beckoned me over with a tilt of his head. "Let's talk," he murmured, leading me away from the group to a quiet corner of the common room. His blue eyes searched mine, seeking the truth that lay beneath scars and walls.

"Tell me about your losses," he said, his voice low, insistent. The command in his tone left no room for evasion. But there were some things I just wasn't ready to share. I felt too ashamed.

"Too many to count," I admitted, the words scraping my throat raw. "The worst... It changed me."

"Mine too," he said, his gaze never leaving mine. "But we're still here."

"Still fighting," I added.

"Exactly." There was a pause, heavy with unspoken understanding. "You're not alone in this fight, Violet. Not anymore."

"Thank you." The gratitude was deep, warming the cold corners of my soul. With March, I didn't need to hide my past.

His nod was solemn.

The room faded away until there was only March, his blue eyes locked onto mine, seeing past the facade to the raw wounds beneath. His jaw clenched, a muscle ticking in his cheek. The silence stretched between us, taut as a wire.

In that quiet, I felt it -- the shift in the air. March's presence enveloped me, the promise of safety wrapping around me like a shield. He didn't need to say the words. His resolve was etched in every line of his body.

"Nobody," he said finally, the word a low growl of protection, "is going to hurt you again. Not on my watch."

"March --" My voice broke.

"Shh." He raised a hand, silencing me. "I mean it. This is personal. I'm surprised Ben didn't come back from the dead to kick my ass when you suffered like that. If I'd kept in touch, maybe things wouldn't have turned out that way. I failed you before. I won't this time."

A guardian angel clad in leather and ink. It almost made me smile. I'd never once blamed him. I'd missed the hell out of him. But deep down, I'd known why he never came back home. For the same reason I hated to remain there. It wasn't the same without Ben.

"I wasn't your responsibility," I said. "I've never once blamed you for the way my life turned out. No one made Ben join the Marines. His death was the result of his choices, not yours."

"We'll have to agree to disagree," March said, briefly closing his eyes.

I nearly reached for him, wanting to offer comfort, but something told me it wouldn't be welcome. No, for now, I'd watch and wait. But if March ever gave any indication he'd welcome my touch, then I wasn't sure I'd be able to hold back.

Chapter Four
Violet

I leaned against the cool counter in the dimly lit clubhouse kitchen, watching Jo stir a pot of something that smelled like heaven. Even the baby in my belly seemed to agree, since I didn't feel like throwing up. Eliza sat at the table, her hands clasped around a steaming mug of tea, her eyes distant yet thoughtful.

"Club life isn't for everyone, Vi," Jo began. "It's about loyalty. Brotherhood -- and sisterhood. You ride with the Underland, you're part of something bigger than yourself. And no, I don't mean we literally ride the way they do. Although, I do enjoy it when Hatter takes me out on his bike. These days, he's worried about the baby, though."

Eliza nodded, her voice barely above a whisper. "It's a bond, unbreakable. We've all been through hell, one way or another. Here... we're safe. We look out for each other. Our men fought in wars, lost people, and some of them have nightmares. Since you knew March before you came here, I'm sure you're already aware of that. But Jo and I both went through our own trauma."

I shifted, uncomfortable with my own vulnerability, yet desperate to understand. "And what about... outside? The dangers?"

Mostly, I wondered if the shit that would follow me would harm everyone here. It hadn't been right to dump my problems on the club. March had been the only person I could think of who could possibly help me, but I'd wondered the entire way here if I was making the right decision.

"Underland's got enemies, sure." Jo's eyes darkened as she glanced toward the window. "But we stand together. Fight together. Protect our own."

Eliza reached across the table, her touch light on my hand. "We're a family, Vi. No one gets left behind. I'm proof enough. The last enemy the club took down was my father, the sheriff. He was rotten and needed to be destroyed, but they still accepted me with open arms."

"Even me?" I asked, the question slipping out. If those men knew Ben, would they want me here? I was a reminder of something awful that happened in their past. Wouldn't seeing me every day just make it worse? I'd often wondered if that's why I hadn't seen March in all these years.

"Especially you," they said in unison.

The warmth from their assurance seeped into my bones. It had already felt like a miracle when March hadn't turned me away. Now these ladies were welcoming me. I couldn't remember the last time I'd felt accepted.

Eliza set her cup aside and picked up a pencil and pad. Her hand moved delicately across the page, and I noticed her fingers were stained with graphite. Jo gave the pot one last stir before joining her. She grabbed the other pad and started to sketch as well. Her strokes seemed bold and confident. Their art was as different as night and day.

"Vi, you ever do any drawing or anything like that?" Eliza asked without lifting her gaze.

"Me? No." I shook my head, feeling a pang of envy. "Never had the knack for it. Or anything artistic for that matter."

"It's just about expression," Jo said, her eyes still on her work. "A release, you know? I also write poetry sometimes."

I nodded, but my mind wandered. My hobbies were more about survival. My brother had taught me the proper way to hold a knife and how to shoot a gun. Not that it had done me any good when I actually needed those skills. I hadn't been armed when I'd needed to be.

Watching them -- their easy camaraderie, their silent understanding -- I felt something twist inside me. These people had chosen each other. Chosen to stand together against whatever darkness chased them. In their world, there was no such thing as a lone wolf. They moved as one pack, fierce and unyielding.

I'd never been part of something like that. Always on the periphery, always looking in. My brother had included me to some extent, but even he'd had his own pals. Like March.

"Vi," Jo began, her voice steady despite the haunted look in her eyes, "you're not on your own here. The Underland MC… it saved me. Saved us. I guess it's kind of what they do. They were heroes before they came to Warren. Maybe they don't know how to turn it off."

Eliza's hand reached out, brushing against mine. "We've all got scars. Some visible, some aren't. Here, they don't define us."

I swallowed hard, feeling the weight of their gazes, the weight of my own past. "I've known March forever. Since we were kids. But to him, I'm just…"

"His best friend's little sister?" Jo supplied, her eyes softening.

"Exactly." My words were barely audible, an ache threading through them. I tried for a wry smile, but it trembled at the edges. How many times had I wished I could be something more to him? Even at the age of eight, I'd wanted to grow up and marry March.

"March is blind then," Eliza said, her voice quiet but firm. "Because you are far too good for him. He'd be lucky to have you."

Their assurance enveloped me, and for a fleeting moment, I allowed myself to believe it.

Something shattered in the other room, and we heard a shout. Jo's hand flew to her rounded belly. Concern flared in me. "Aren't you scared?" I blurted out, motioning to her stomach. "To bring a baby into… all this?"

Jo's laughter was a surprise, warm and unafraid. "Sometimes, yeah. I dream of a house with a yard, somewhere safe for little feet to run. But this place is home. Besides, where else would you get a bunch of tough bikers to change a diaper?"

The idea brought a genuine laugh from me. Maybe there was room here for new life, for hope amid the hardened exteriors.

It wasn't traditional, but perhaps it was exactly what we needed.

"Actually." Eliza's cheeks flushed, and she glanced down at her own midsection. "I'm expecting too. We haven't told anyone. Until now."

My gaze snapped to her. "You are?"

Nodding, Eliza tucked a stray lock of hair behind her ear, her movements gentle. "Cheshire knows. We've been talking about getting a little house close by. Someplace… just ours. But he's worried. Being out there, even if it's close… it could make us vulnerable."

"Targets," I whispered. The world outside these walls wasn't kind. And March had said something about corrupt officials. Just how unsafe was the town of Warren? I'd thought, being such a small place, it would be more like those fifties TV shows.

"Exactly." Her fingers traced an invisible line on the tabletop.

I thought of my own situation, the tiny heartbeat

growing stronger inside me, the heartbeat that had driven me here, to this unlikely sanctuary. My voice wavered as I added my truth to theirs. "I'm pregnant too."

Their heads turned, whiskey and sky-colored eyes meeting mine. A shared understanding passed between us -- three women, three futures taking shape beneath the protective shadow of the club.

"Does March know?" Jo's question was gentle, but it pierced the heart of my deepest wishes.

"March?" I laughed, though it sounded more like a choke. "Yeah. He knows. But it's not like the baby is his. He's always been out of reach. Probably always will be."

"But you'd like him to be the dad?" Eliza asked.

"Wouldn't he be wonderful?" The admission spilled from me, a fantasy I'd nurtured in the quiet corners of my mind, never daring to give it voice until now. "I've always thought he was great with children. I don't think he sees himself that way, though."

"Violet." Jo reached over, her hand warm atop mine. "You never know what might happen."

"In this place, things have a way of surprising you." Eliza smiled.

I shook my head. "In another life, maybe."

But as I said it, I let myself steal a glance through the doorway, where March laughed with Cheshire and Hatter, so full of life and strength. And in that moment, foolish or not, I embraced the warmth that flooded through me, the ember of hope that refused to die. What if they were right? What if I really did have a chance?

Jo's hand still rested gently on mine, and it felt like she was trying to anchor me. I looked around, taking in the clubhouse kitchen. It seemed homey, considering it belonged in a biker clubhouse. I wondered if these women had something to do with it, or if March and the others had decorated this place before the women came here.

Eliza's eyes were soft with almost a haunted look to them. "This place changes you."

"Changes how?" I asked.

"It gives you roots," Jo interjected, her other hand resting on the swell of her belly. "And wings, all at once. The men are protective but try not to stifle us. At the same time, they want to keep us safe. Considering my past trauma, it doesn't bother me, but to some it might seem smothering."

"Roots and wings," I repeated. Could I have that too if I stayed here? Would March even let me? These women were with Hatter and Cheshire. Things were different for them.

"Exactly," she affirmed. "Here, you're never just drifting. You're part of something bigger."

My heart swelled with gratitude that they seemed to be fine with me being part of the Underland MC family. Welcoming, even. The raucous laughter from the main room filtered through, not as a disruption but as a reminder of the vitality that thrummed through this place.

"Thank you," I whispered, not sure if they understood just how deeply I meant it. The safety of this refuge enveloped me.

"Anytime," Jo said, giving my hand a reassuring squeeze. "We stick together here."

Eliza nodded in agreement, her hand mirroring Jo's gesture. "We've all got scars. It's what we do with them that counts."

Scars. Yes, I had those -- some visible, most not. But here, among these women who'd seen their fair share of battles, I felt a kinship that went beyond common fears and whispered dreams. This was a sanctuary, a place where my vulnerability didn't feel like a liability.

Resolve hardened within me. I would do more than survive. I would thrive -- for me, for the tiny life inside me. I would learn to navigate this world and find my place among them. Even if March wouldn't let me stay indefinitely, it didn't mean I had to leave Warren. I could remain in this town, be friends with these women, and start a new life. I wanted to become someone I could be proud of, and I really hoped I could be a good mom. I couldn't blame my baby for their father's part in their creation.

I got up and moved to the doorway, leaning against the frame. I watched March. His laughter blended with the cacophony of clinking glasses and a throaty engine somewhere nearby. Cheshire threw his head back, his grin slicing through the dim light. Beside him, Hatter's chuckle rumbled like distant thunder.

The warmth spread from the core of my being, tingling in my fingertips. I sipped it in, this strange cocktail of affection and longing. It felt dangerous, addictive. March caught someone's joke, and his eyes crinkled at the corners. Seeing him like this, so carefree, stirred something in me. Something deep. When had I ever seen that expression on his face?

I bit down on my lip, tasting the ghost of a smile. What was this feeling? This pull toward him, magnetic and undeniable? If I'd had a crush on the man before, I was starting to worry I might be halfway in love with him now. Seeing this version of him made me want things I shouldn't. I needed to remind myself that a life with March would probably never be more than just a dream.

But as I stood there, hidden in the shadows, March's gaze swung in my direction. Our eyes locked. The air hitched in my throat, my heart skipped. In that split second of silence, I saw him. Not the biker, not my brother's friend, but March. The boy who had always been there, blurred now into the man before me.

He nodded at me, a simple gesture that probably didn't mean much to him, but right then I knew. It wasn't just a crush that had tethered me to him all these years. It was more, much more.

Could I have loved him all along?

The thought sent a shiver down my spine, a secret thrill that danced across my skin. I looked away, cheeks burning. But inside, I held onto that look, that fleeting connection.

"Hey," Jo called out softly from behind, pulling me from my reverie.

"Hey," I managed back, still clutching the doorway for support.

"Come join us," she urged, her hand gentle on my shoulder.

I glanced back at March, Cheshire, and Hatter -- the trio now embroiled in some animated story that had everyone around them leaning in. Strength coursed through me, a surge of courage borne from the women who'd welcomed me and the man who unknowingly held my heart.

"Okay," I said, stepping forward. My voice was barely above a whisper, but it carried the weight of my resolution.

Whatever it took. Whatever my heart desired. I was ready. For the Underland MC, for my baby, for March.

And perhaps, just maybe, for love.

Chapter Five
March

I'd stepped out to get some air, feeling as if the walls were pressing in on me. Rain poured and I watched the lightning flash in the distance. As I stared out at the trees around the property, a slight movement caught my attention. Squinting, I watched the shadows and saw it again. It was too small to be a human. What the hell was out there?

Stepping out into the deluge, I approached whatever was moving around, low to the ground. When I got closer, I realized it was a baby animal. No, not just any animal... a kitten. Large eyes stared at me as the pitiful creature opened its mouth and let out a silent meow. Its legs were mired in the mud, and I gently extracted it.

The small creature shivered in my palm as I cradled it close to my chest. Hurrying inside, I took it straight to my room and started a warm shower. I knew it was risky, since the water might make it panic, but I had to get it cleaned up -- and warm. I'd have used the sink, but I worried the heavier stream of water might scare it even more. At least the shower would be more like rain.

"It's all right, little one." Once the water was the right temperature, I quickly rinsed the mud from its fur. It eventually stopped shaking, so I wrapped it in a towel and wondered what the hell I was going to do with it.

I opened the footlocker at the end of my bed and pulled out everything but a blanket. Spreading it across the bottom, I set the kitten down and went to the kitchen to figure something out for it. Never having had a pet before, I didn't know what it could or couldn't eat, didn't have a clue how old it was, or anything else. But leaving it in the storm had been out of the question.

Raiding the fridge, I found some leftover baked chicken and sliced off small pieces, then shredded it. As tiny as it was, I wasn't even sure if it would eat regular food. Did it need formula like a baby?

"What the hell are you doing?" Hatter asked, eying the small amount of shredded meat I'd placed on a paper towel.

"Found a kitten. Clearly, I'm not leaving to go get cat stuff in this storm, so I thought I'd give it some chicken."

Hatter arched a brow and grunted. "Fine. You'll need to give it water too. But if that thing escapes your room and starts shitting everywhere, *you're* cleaning the clubhouse."

I didn't think it could escape the footlocker, so I wasn't worried about that. Although, now that he'd mentioned it shitting… fuck. I noticed a stack of Amazon boxes in the corner of the kitchen, probably courtesy of Eliza and Jo, and grabbed the smallest one, then I shredded some paper towel into the bottom. Hatter handed me the lid off an empty peanut butter jar.

"What's this for?" I asked.

"Water," he said. "If it's small, I doubt it can drink out of one of our bowls. And judging by the size of the makeshift litter box you just made, it's fucking small as hell."

I nodded. "Yep."

I gathered up everything and took it to my room. The kitten cried pitifully from inside the footlocker. I put the litter box in one corner and the food and water on the other side. At first, it just stared at me. Then its nose started to twitch, and it stumbled a bit before finding the chicken.

Satisfied it wouldn't starve to death overnight, I went into the bathroom to clean up. I didn't know what the hell I was going to do with the little cat, but I'd figure it out tomorrow. For now, it was safe and would have a full belly. That would be enough.

I left the little critter to settle in and grabbed a beer before taking a seat in the common room. Tweedle came over and claimed the spot beside me.

"So, what was that earlier?" he asked.

"Found a kitten outside. Couldn't leave it there to die." I shrugged. I didn't understand why everyone was making a big deal out of it. They would have done the same.

Tweedle took a swallow of his beer and watched me. "Never took you for the type to have a cat."

"Didn't say I was keeping it."

Tweedle snorted. "Yeah, right. You're going to what… abandon it at a shelter? Not likely. Whether you admit it or not, that cat is yours now."

Fucking hell. I had a feeling he was right. Just what I needed. There was enough on my plate already.

* * *

Word had spread fast about the little furball in my room. To everyone except Violet. She'd been absent all day, and I was worried about her.

I pushed open the door to Vi's room, the silence hanging heavy. There she was, perched on the edge of the bed, a lone figure drowning in thought. Her dark hair spilled over her shoulders, a stark contrast against the pale sheets.

"March." Vi's voice broke through the stillness. The depth of sadness in her whiskey-colored eyes snagged me, held me captive. She patted the space beside her, an unspoken plea etched into her features.

"Sit with me?"

Stepping forward felt like wading through molasses, each step heavier than the last. I took my place beside her, close enough to feel the warmth radiating from her skin.

"Thanks for coming," she said.

"Missed you today. Seems like you've been holed up in here all day. I got worried," I said.

I hovered at the edge of indecision, muscles coiled tight. The room felt smaller, walls closing in with the ghosts of a past I struggled to keep caged. Ben's face flashed behind my eyelids, always there, a specter that knew no rest. It felt wrong, being here with Violet. At the same time, if I'd kept tabs on her, maybe something awful wouldn't have happened to her.

"March?" Vi's tentative voice pulled me back to the present.

"Sorry." I exhaled a shaky breath. My hands rested on my thighs, fingers digging into the denim as if I could anchor myself in the now.

She turned toward me, her delicate features shadowed by grief. "It's been hard," she started, the words catching like burrs in her throat. "Since... since Ben left us."

"Vi..." I wanted to reach out, to bridge the gap with touch, but fear rooted me in place. I didn't have the right to console her, to touch her.

"Every day, it's like walking through a fog. I keep thinking he'll just come strolling in, you know? That smile of his lighting up the room." Her voice trembled, the laughter that should've accompanied the memory was absent, stolen by sorrow.

"Sounds like Ben," I murmured.

"Everyone keeps telling me it gets easier." She

drew in a ragged breath, her eyes glistening with unshed tears. "But they're not the ones waking up to the emptiness where he used to be. It's been years, and it still hurts just as much today as it did when I first found out he was gone."

Her pain echoed mine, a mirror reflecting an ache so deep it hollowed out the soul. I clenched my fists, nails biting into my palms, the sting a welcome distraction from the void that threatened to swallow me whole.

"Doesn't feel like it gets easier, does it?" I knew how she felt, except I had a large dose of guilt added to my suffering. I'd been right there. Watched him fall. What if I could have stopped it from happening? I'd asked myself that a million times.

"No, it doesn't." Her gaze met mine.

"Every night, it's just darkness," Vi whispered. "Did you ever get over it?"

There was a plea in her eyes, searching for an answer I wasn't sure I had. Did she want me to move past it? Or was she hoping I'd dwell in the past, live buried in pain, for the rest of my life?

"Over it?" The question hung heavy, a challenge to my composure.

"His death. The pain." She held her breath.

"Never." The word was final, a sentence passed down without appeal. "It's always there. Like a shadow."

A sigh had her shoulders slumping. "I thought so. You know it's not your fault. He wouldn't have blamed you, and neither do I." Her hand fluttered near mine, not touching, just existing in the space between.

"Isn't it?" The question was for me more than her. Regret bled into my tone.

"Ben made his choice." Her words were gentle,

but they cut through me, stark and true. "No one forced him to enlist. He did that all on his own, and he knew the risks."

"Choices…" Yeah, no one had made him join, but would he have considered it if I hadn't already signed my papers? He'd wanted to go with me, to see foreign lands.

My hands clenched into fists at my sides, knuckles whitening with the strain. The muscles along my jaw tensed. Violet reached out her hand, hesitating for just a moment before resting it gently on my arm. It was a touch meant to soothe, to heal. The warmth of her skin bled through the fabric of my shirt, seeping into the cold recesses of my guarded heart.

"Hey," she whispered, her fingers light but insistent against the muscle coiled tight beneath them. "It's okay."

"Is it?" The words were a growl, born from a place of raw pain I seldom let anyone see.

"Talk to me," she urged, her grip tightening ever so slightly, grounding me. "Please."

Her plea didn't need volume to resonate. It carried the weight of shared grief, a bridge spanning the gap between us. I looked down at our arms, at the stark contrast of her delicate fingers wrapped around the bulk of my forearm. In that simple gesture, she offered more than comfort -- she offered a chance at absolution. And for the first time, I considered taking it.

Raising my gaze to meet hers, I braced for the storm. The accusation. The anger. Ben's ghost hovered between us. If he'd lived, this would have probably been his room. I couldn't bring myself to tell her that.

But Vi's eyes… they didn't carry the tempest I expected. They were calm pools reflecting not the past but the here and now. In them, I saw something that unnerved me more than rage ever could: understanding. And beneath that, a well of forgiveness so deep it threatened to wash away the fortress I'd built around myself.

Her touch, still resting on my arm, ignited a firestorm of sensation that blistered through my defenses. A warmth that had no place in the cold order of my life spread from the point of contact, sending shockwaves through my system. My heart kicked against my chest, a caged beast desperate for release.

"Your pain," she started, her tone threading through the chaos of my thoughts, "it's mine too."

The words landed, heavy and true. We were allies in sorrow, bound by a history that both united and divided us. The world outside faded. It all slipped away until there was nothing but the weight of her hand on my arm and the silent promise that lingered in her touch.

My eyes refused to break away from her. She wasn't that little girl anymore, the one who used to tag along behind me and Ben, eyes wide with hero worship. That girl was gone, stripped away by time and tragedy. The woman who had taken her place mesmerized me. She was vulnerable, yes. But she had a strength that radiated from her. She shone brilliantly, like the sun. It hurt to look too long, but you couldn't help it. You just had to see the light.

"Are you okay?" The concern etched in her features was for me. Me, who should be the rock, the protector.

"Fine," I lied, my voice betraying none of the turmoil. "You know, when my mind is chaotic, or I start feeling suffocated, I go for a ride. No idea if you've ever been on a motorcycle, but we can give it a try sometime. If you want to."

She smiled a little. "I think I'd like that."

Her fingers brushed against mine, a whisper of contact that sent another shockwave through me. She was strength wrapped in softness, a paradox.

What could I say? That I wanted her? That she shouldn't be touching me like this? I glanced at her hand where it still touched. I couldn't bring myself to put my thoughts into words, too scared she'd move away.

I wanted her. Gods, I wanted her in ways I never thought I'd want anything again. But this was Vi -- Ben's sister, the girl I should have protected.

We were silent, communicating through the tension that crackled between us. Every breath, every heartbeat, felt like a declaration. And I was a man who didn't know how to read the signs. What did she want from me? And was it something I was even able to give her?

I took a deep breath, the air heavy. "There's guilt eating me alive. You say it wasn't my fault, but I can't help but wonder if I'd done something differently, I could have changed what happened."

Her body stilled, the bed creaking under our combined weight. Her whiskey eyes widened, brimming with a silent question, waiting.

"Ben was my brother in all but blood," I continued. "And I --"

"March, you don't have to," she pleaded softly, her hand finding mine.

"Need to. You should know." My fingers wrapped around hers, squeezing until the truth spilled out of me. "I couldn't save him. And now... seeing you here, needing me -- it's like facing a ghost. He would have wanted me to keep an eye on you. Instead, I ran because I felt so fucking guilty. He died right beside me. What if I'd been standing there instead? What if I'd noticed the sniper in time?"

"Stop." There was steel in her voice now. "You're not to blame for Ben. And I'm not a ghost -- I'm right here."

"You're becoming more to me than Ben's little sister. And I don't know if I can -- should -- let that happen."

"You're more to me too. More than Ben's friend. Always have been."

"Always?" Did she really mean that?

"Always," she confirmed, and in her eyes, I saw the reflection of my own heart laid bare.

The air between us thickened as we sat side by side. Her hand was still in mine, warmth seeping into my calloused skin. The room shrank around us. Vi shifted, her leg brushing against mine. Electricity sparked. My heart raced, betraying the calm I fought to maintain. She was here. Not a ghost, but flesh and bone -- flesh and bone that could be broken. Or cherished. And that's what I wanted to do. Cherish her.

"Where do we go from here?" she asked.

"Forward," I said. "Together."

"Can we?" Doubt shadowed her features, lines of worry etching into her forehead.

"Have to try." I squeezed her hand. "If you're willing, that is."

She gave a little nod, and some of the tension inside me eased. Even though we were now on the same page, I still felt a little lost. Not in a million years had I ever pictured this scenario.

"Scared?" she asked.

"Terrified," I admitted.

"Me too," she confessed, leaning into me.

Our silence returned, but now it felt different -- charged with possibility.

Chapter Six
Violet

My arms tightened around March's waist, not just for safety, but from a longing that was terrifying. I buried my face against his back, drinking in the scent of leather and something woodsy that clung to him like a second skin. He was the epitome of strength. But then he always had been, even when he was just a teenager.

"Hold on tighter," he commanded over the wind's howl. I felt the vibration of him speaking, and it made me want to cuddle even closer.

We rode fast, the world around us a blur of green and gray as we sliced through the countryside. The thrum of the bike beneath us was like a living thing, a wild beast that March tamed with an expert hand. Each shift, each turn, I felt more attuned to him, our bodies moving in sync as if we were extensions of each other.

Later, after we'd ridden for at least an hour, we found ourselves in the dimly lit garage, alone amidst the scattered parts and gleaming motorcycles. March had said he'd teach me about bikes if I wanted to learn. It wasn't so much the lesson I looked forward to, but just spending time with him.

The darkness settled around us. I clutched my jacket tighter, the chill of the evening air seeping into my bones.

"Are you cold?" March rubbed his hands up and down my arms.

"A bit," I admitted.

"We should head inside. Besides, I need to check on the little furball." He tipped his head toward the clubhouse.

"Fur... what?" My brow furrowed. "What are

you talking about"?"

He grabbed the back of his neck. "Shit. Guess I didn't tell you. I found a stray kitten in the storm. Poor thing was covered in mud and shivering. It's in my room right now. I need to go out tomorrow and get a few things while I decide what to do with it. I had a small bag of food and a dish delivered, but if I'm going to keep it longer, it needs more things."

A kitten? I bit my lip so I wouldn't smile. I could easily see the big guy with a tiny poof ball of a cat. Even though he'd never had a pet, he'd always been good with animals. Stray dogs would go up to him for attention. If he went to someone's house and they had animals, they'd cling to March. People too for that matter. I'd always admired the ease with which he approached life. Maybe things had changed after Ben died, but before that, March had been a different person. I was happy to see at least this part of him hadn't changed.

He led me to his room and pointed to the footlocker at the end of the bed. I noticed the lid was open. "I put it in there. Didn't want it getting stuck under the furniture or escaping the room."

I hurried over and peered inside. Big golden eyes stared up at me. It didn't look very old, but its fur was already floofy, and a beautiful silver color. I noticed it had two white toes and a white tip on its tail.

"Oh, my goodness! It's beautiful!" I reached down and paused. "Can I hold it?"

"Sure."

The moment my hand got close to it, the kitten started bouncing around the space, going straight into play mode. I couldn't help but laugh as all four paws came up off the bottom of the footlocker. "It hops like a bunny!"

He peered down at it and grunted. "So, what? I should call it bunny or something ridiculous?"

"Rabbit wouldn't like sharing a name with it. Can't call it Tigger since it isn't orange. What else bounces?"

He shrugged. "A ball?"

I couldn't contain my laughter this time and laughed until tears slipped down my cheeks. "You can't call it ball."

"Then you name it," he said. "I was never good at naming things."

I studied the little thing. "Any idea if it's a girl or boy?"

"I didn't check, and I have no idea if it's too early to tell. Are cats one of those creatures that you can't sex easily until they're older?"

"Google it," I said, and reached down again, this time lifting the kitten and holding it against my chest. It started to softly chew on my hand and purr. I melted, and knew I had to talk March into keeping it.

"Flip it over and let me look," he said. I turned the kitten onto its back and scratched its chest while March checked to see what gender it was. "Looks like a girl."

"Then what about Luna? She's silver like moonlight."

He nodded. "Works for me. Luna it is. Wait. Does this mean I'm keeping that thing?"

"Yep. Congratulations. You're now a cat daddy."

He rubbed a hand down his face. "Fantastic."

He could grumble all he wanted, but I knew he wasn't really upset about it. If he had been, the kitten wouldn't have been here in his room. He'd have fobbed it off on someone else.

I set the kitten back into the makeshift pen and

turned to face March. Without warning, he closed the distance, his arms enveloping me in an embrace that stole my breath away. A hug shouldn't have made me feel so many things, but it did.

"Thanks for today," I whispered.

"Any time."

Something told me he meant it. Although, once I was more noticeably pregnant, it probably wouldn't be a good idea for me to ride on his motorcycle. It had been so much fun, so freeing. I'd never experienced anything like it before.

"You should get some rest," he said, taking a step back.

"What if I don't want to?" I asked, feeling brave for a moment. I'd spent my entire life just surviving. My brother had always kept me safe. I had no idea how much he'd shared with March, but once Ben left, things at home weren't so great. I no longer had my shield. I wanted something more now, a life with March. But I had a feeling if I didn't reach out to grab it, he'd slip right through my fingers. Eventually, he'd start feeling guilty again.

I lurched forward, intent on grabbing hold of him, but instead I tripped and fell into him. March's arms came around me, holding me close. I dared to lift my gaze to his, finding not the usual reserve, but a flicker of something else -- something that mirrored the heat coursing through me.

"Thanks." My body was still pressed to his, and I wasn't ready to back up anytime soon.

"Careful, Vi." The corner of his mouth twitched, a ghost of a smile that sent my pulse racing.

His hands lingered at my waist, and my heart pounded so furiously I was certain he could feel it. In his hold, I found both safety and danger, a paradox that defined the world I had come to inhabit -- his world.

"March," I began, my nerves alight, "there's something I need to tell you."

The world narrowed to the space between us. His breath mingled with mine. His hands, still at my waist, held me as if I were something precious, not the mess of nerves and longing that I was. I couldn't hold back any longer.

Driven by a courage I didn't know I had, I rose on tiptoe. My lips found his in a tentative touch, a whisper of a kiss that held every silent word I'd ever wanted to say.

His body stiffened with shock, a statue under my touch. I could taste the surprise on him in the sharp intake of his breath. But I didn't draw back. Couldn't.

Just when I thought he'd pull away, he responded. March's lips moved against mine with a gentleness that belied his rugged exterior. The kiss deepened, and I felt him, truly felt him -- every barrier he'd erected, every guarded secret, melted away under the heat of our connection.

"Vi," he murmured against my mouth. His arms tightened around me, pulling me closer until there was no space left for doubt or fear. His kiss was a revelation, an unspoken promise.

I clung to him, fingers gripping the leather of his cut, as if I could anchor myself in the storm of emotions he'd unleashed within me. And in that instant, his kiss spoke louder than any words could -- it said he felt it too.

March's kiss scorched through the chill of the night, igniting a fire that spread with reckless abandon. His lips, once hesitant, now ravaged mine with a fervor that left me breathless and desperate for more. The urgency in his touch spoke of raw need, a hunger too long denied and now unleashed.

This wasn't just a kiss. It was so much more.

His hands roamed my back, strong and unyielding, pressing me into the solid wall of his chest. My fingers tangled in his short hair, the coarse strands a stark contrast to the tenderness of his touch. Each nip and caress was a brand, marking me as irrevocably his.

The world outside faded. The taste of him -- whiskey and wild freedom -- consumed my senses, leaving no room for thought, only feeling.

"More," I whispered against his lips, the word breaking on a shudder. March obliged, deepening the kiss until I was drowning in sensation, every nerve alight with the storm he'd summoned.

The passion that flared between us was relentless, an unstoppable force that neither of us had the will to resist. As the kiss finally slowed, a sense of peace settled over me. We lingered there, on the precipice of something monumental, the weight of what this moment meant hanging heavy in the air.

"Stay with me tonight," March whispered, his voice hoarse with emotion. How could I ever tell him no? He was offering the one thing I'd always wanted -- him.

"When you say stay, you mean..."

He lightly traced over my collarbone, his touch making me shiver. He leaned in closer, his lips near my ear. "I want you, Violet. You look positively delicious, and I want a taste."

My knees nearly gave out. If he hadn't had a good hold of me, I'd have been on the floor. March backed me to the wall and pinned my hands over my head, leaving no doubt as to who was in charge. A thrill ran through me at his dominance. This was what

I had been craving for so long. Without permission or consent from me, he reached down to pop open the button on my jeans. The rasp of the zipper was loud in the otherwise quiet room.

With anyone else, I may have panicked. But this was March. The way he studied me, I knew he was watching for any sign I might freak out. I trusted him completely. Had absolute faith he'd never harm me. I hoped he could see all that shining in my eyes.

He slipped his hand inside my jeans, delving between my legs. His fingers stroked my pussy through my panties, and I thought my heart might burst from my chest.

"Oh, fuck yes!"

He groaned while pushing me against the wall. March pulled his hand free and his hips ground against mine teasingly, making sure I felt how hard he was, how much he wanted me.

"Tell me no, Vi. It's now or never. If we go any further, I won't be in control anymore. There won't be any stopping me."

I held his gaze, and tried to show him how sincere I was with my answer. "I don't want you to stop, Marcus. You're the only man I've ever wanted. If you told me to leave right now, I think I'd cry."

"Well, we can't have that now, can we?" He backed up and helped me strip out of my clothes. I fought the urge to cover myself, and instead let him look his fill. As his gaze hungrily devoured me, he removed his clothes.

I'd known he was big -- everywhere -- but my imagination hadn't done him justice. He was... "Beautiful."

He chuckled. "I think that's my line."

I reached out to trace a finger over the bulldog

tattoo on his bicep. "Devil dog."

He didn't stop me, so I kept exploring. My eyes misted with tears when I saw the dog tags over his heart. They were Ben's. All this time, he'd carried my brother with him.

A line in script across his ribs was unfamiliar to me. I glanced up, hoping he'd tell me what it meant.

"Marine Corps hymn."

He turned and I placed my hand over the club colors for the Underland MC. But scattered around it were dog tags, each for a member of the club. *Always faithful* was in rough font below it on his lower back. This man lived and breathed for other people. I knew without a doubt he'd give his life for this club. They weren't anything like the ones I'd seen on TV. Instead, they'd created something of their own.

He turned to face me again. Without a word, I reached for him. He took my hand and led me to the bed, following me down onto the mattress. I'd had quite a few regrets in my life, but I knew this would never be one of them.

His body hovered over mine. His hand found its way to my inner thigh, teasingly inching closer to my pussy. My breath hitched as he slipped a finger inside me.

"Tell me what you want," he growled, his voice rough and demanding. His other hand gripped my hair tightly, forcing my face closer to his. The heat between us was palpable, undeniable.

"I want you to fuck me," I whispered, each word quivering with desire. "Don't hold back, Marcus. I want all of you. The good, bad, and ugly."

He chuckled darkly. "You may get more than you bargained for, baby girl. You're fucking beautiful. Not sure I'm capable of holding back."

As if to prove his point, he lowered his head and claimed my mouth with his, igniting a fiery need within me. His tongue danced with mine, teasing and exploring every inch of my mouth. I could feel his cock pressing against me, eager for entrance.

I reached up to touch his chest, feeling the hard muscle beneath my fingertips. "I belong to you," I whispered, my voice shaking. "I always have."

His response was swift and shocking. He grabbed my hair and pulled my head back, exposing my neck. His hot breath fanned across my skin as he growled, and bit down on my shoulder. I cried out from surprise, but heat unfurled inside me. I'd never have guessed there was such a feral side to him, but I loved it. I arched my back instinctively, needing more.

Without warning, I felt the press of his cock as he slowly entered me. My pussy burned and throbbed as I stretched to accommodate him. He moved slowly, as if savoring the moment. I couldn't hold back my moan, and it seemed to make March snap. With a low growl, he began thrusting into me like a man possessed. The headboard slammed against the wall, and still it wasn't enough.

"Please, Marcus," I begged. "Harder."

He lifted up a little, his gaze finding mine. As I stared into his eyes, he owned every inch of me, laying claim to me in the most thorough way possible. My hips lifted to meet his, our bodies moving in a rhythmic dance of pleasure. I didn't think I'd last much longer, and he seemed to know it.

March gripped my hip and changed the angle of his thrusts. He hit just the right spot again and again, until I saw stars. I came, screaming his name, and wishing this moment would never end. He drove into me with almost punishing strokes, and I felt his cock harden even more. He grunted as he pumped his hot cum into me, not slowing until the very end.

"Marcus, I... that was..."

He kissed me softly. "I should have been gentler."

I shook my head. "It was perfect. And if you're worried because of what happened to me, you shouldn't. I knew it was you the entire time, and I wasn't the least bit scared. This is nothing like what I went through."

His gaze narrowed. "If I'd seen even one hint of fear in your eyes, or hesitation, you know I'd have stopped, right? But I worried asking would take you out of the moment between us and put you right back in the nightmare you're trying so hard to get past."

I reached up to touch his cheek. "I figured as much. The way you watched me told me everything I needed to know."

"You're amazing, Vi. You know this changes things, right?"

I nodded. "I'm okay with that. Are you?"

He flashed me a smile. "Yeah. I'm more than okay with it."

Marcus collapsed onto the bed beside me, and I snuggled into his side. I didn't know what our lives would look like from this point onward, but as long as he was beside me, I didn't care. Right now, I had everything I'd ever dreamed of, and I never wanted to let go.

Chapter Seven
Violet

The hum of my computer filled the room. Absolem leaned over a stack of documents, his glasses perched on the bridge of his nose. He'd filled me in on everything, and I'd reviewed the papers he had spread out in this room. They'd apparently made a "war" room.

"All right," he began, his voice low and steady. "We've got one shot at this."

I nodded, feeling the weight of my responsibility knotting in my stomach. My fingers danced across the keyboard, the keys click-clacking under my touch. His blue eyes met mine, serious and unwavering.

"Your skills," he said, pointing to my laptop, "are the key. We need proof of every shady deal Davis and Lewis have their hands in. I've shown you what I found so far. I need to see if you can dig up more."

"Got it. Digging through digital dirt is my specialty."

"Remember, we don't want them to see us coming," Absolem added.

I turned to my screen, the green cursor blinking back at me. It was go time. I cracked my knuckles, my heart thudding against my ribs as if trying to break free. This wasn't just about me anymore. Warren was going to be my home, and I wanted to make sure my child had a safe place to grow up. We needed to end the corruption.

"Accessing city's database now," I murmured, typing furiously, lines of code flowing from my mind to my fingertips. The familiar rush of adrenaline surged as firewalls fell before me, one by one.

"Security's tight," I noted, the challenge sparking

excitement in my veins. "But not tight enough."

"Keep pushing," Absolem encouraged.

Lines of code cascaded down my screen, a matrix only I could decipher. I was in, deeper into the city's protected files than anyone outside the government should ever be. Transactions, communications, records -- all laid bare before me.

"Looking for anything out of place," I told him, scanning the numbers that represented a darker reality. Each entry, each transfer was a potential piece of the puzzle we desperately needed to complete.

"Time's not on our side," Absolem reminded me, without needing to look at his watch.

"Understood," I replied, my focus razor-sharp.

Then, there it was, hidden amidst the mundane -- a series of transactions that didn't belong. Numbers that screamed dirty money, a paper trail leading straight to the top.

"Absolem," I said. "I think I've got something."

Absolem was already on his feet. I kept going, hoping I'd found something really big this time. My neck felt tense and my back ached, which told me more time had passed than I'd realized. Sweat dripped down my spine as I found a shell company, and overseas bank account, and the names of dozens of women and girls.

My gut clenched when I realized the mayor had not only had a hand in selling them, but he'd also purchased some. As quickly as he went through them, I knew something far worse had happened to them. It took me another hour to stumble across an email he'd sent to Lewis... about getting rid of a body. We had him! Proof he'd murdered one of the girls.

"Here!" I showed Absolem. "Is this what you needed? He's not only into the trafficking ring the sheriff was running, but he bought some of the girls. All underage. And he's murdered at least one of them. If I had to guess, I'd say they're all dead."

"Yes. That's what we needed." He patted my shoulder. "Good work. Now get the fuck out of there before someone discovers you nosing around."

Once I saved the evidence I'd found, I did as he said, my hands dancing across the keyboard. Before I completely backed out, there was one more thing I wanted to check. As I went in another direction, I realized my hunch was right. He'd also been bribed, many times.

"Gotcha!" If they couldn't take him down for the murder and rape of underage girls, then I knew no one in this town would be able to ignore *this*. The emails were damning, conversations detailing illegal activities with a casual indifference that made my blood boil. Each message, another nail in their coffins, hammered home by their own hands.

"Violet? Jesus! I told you to get out there!" Absolem said.

"I wanted more, and I found it. You'll have copies of everything."

"I'll get it to the interim sheriff. He helped us take down the last sheriff, so I know we can trust him. He wants Warren to be a safe place to live."

I nodded. "If you think he's trustworthy, that's all that matters."

"You still aren't out of there!"

"Check this out." I turned my screen so he could see the camera feed I'd hacked into. Bonus, it included sound!

The mayor entered the underground area, his gait reeking of arrogance. Behind him, a crime boss I'd seen on TV before loomed. Their voices unfurled through the laptop speakers.

"Thirty percent cut. You get us the contract, Davis," growled the crime boss, his hand extending.

"Consider it done. This city is mine to carve up," the mayor boasted, his palm meeting the crime boss's in a clasp thick with sin.

"Recording this by the way," I said.

"Good."

The meeting's final words slithered through the speakers. As the two parted ways, I stopped recording and backed out of the security system. I snapped my laptop shut. "It's done. You should have enough to take him down."

"I'll call Park Hurst."

I saw the look of determination on his face, and I knew Absolem was going to do whatever it took to get rid of the mayor and his sidekick. "Be careful."

"Always am." There was a hint of a smile in his voice, but it was gone as quickly as it appeared. He placed the phone to his ear, and I heard the murmur of someone answering on the other end.

"Hurst, it's Absolem. We need to meet." He paused and I could tell he was listening to the man say something. "More than *something*. It's time to take down the mayor and Lewis."

Absolem killed the call, his blue eyes locking with mine. A silent vow passed between us, a promise to see this through to the bitter end, whatever it took. For justice. For the club. For our future.

"Got the last of the financial records," I muttered, dragging the files into an encrypted folder. "They thought they were clever, hiding it all behind shell companies."

"Good work. Let's summarize the key points for Hurst. Keep it clear, irrefutable. He likes things neat and simple."

"Right." My heart hammered. We worked in tandem, compiling the report. I gave Absolem all the details and he helped condense it. Hours later, we'd reduced a stack of documents into a two-page report.

It was time to bring down the mayor and Lewis.

* * *

I hadn't thought he would take me with him when he met the interim sheriff. Even more surprising, March had allowed it. I'd thought for sure he would throw a fit about needing to keep me safe. Or perhaps he knew Absolem wouldn't let anything happen to me.

We sat across from Interim Sheriff Hurst, the fluorescent lights of the precinct casting stark shadows across his square jaw. His eyes flicked through the report, green depths stormy with the weight of what he read.

"Mayor Davis is neck-deep," Hurst grumbled, setting the papers down. "And Lewis isn't far behind him. How reliable is your evidence?"

"Rock-solid," Absolem stated, his tone leaving no room for doubt. "Surveillance, firsthand accounts, financial trails. It's all there. And… Violet found an email between the mayor and Lewis about needing to get rid of the body of one of the girls. It's pretty clear he killed her, and there's mention of her age."

"Warren's been under Davis's thumb too long. It's time for that to end." He stood, determination etching lines into his face. "I'll need to pull in some favors, make sure this sticks."

"Whatever it takes," Absolem agreed, his grip tightening on my hand. "We're in this until the end."

"Good." Hurst's nod was curt. "I'll get things moving. Expect heat from Davis's camp but hold steady. We're going to clean up this town."

"Count on it," Absolem said.

The room felt colder suddenly, as if the air had dropped ten degrees within seconds. Hurst's eyes darted to the door, then back to us, his posture rigid.

"Something isn't right," he said, voice low, an edge of warning to it.

Absolem tensed. "What do you mean?"

"I think someone knows we're meeting. Knows about your investigation. Until now, I didn't think they suspected me being part of all this. I tried to lie low and act surprised when the previous sheriff disappeared. Now I'm not sure I was convincing." Hurst's green eyes flickered with something I couldn't place -- fear, maybe? Betrayal?

"Who?" Absolem's question was sharp.

"Can't say. But it's bad." Hurst swallowed hard.

"Spit it out, Park," Absolem growled.

"I didn't want to say anything until I knew for sure, but I've heard they're planning a hit. On the club. Tonight." Hurst glanced at me then Absolem. "Do you understand? This time will be different. They want you all dead."

"Damn it! We need to move. Now!"

"Underland is in their sights. Did we lead them there?" My throat felt like it was closing up. "Did *I* do this?"

Sure, the club had been trying to take down the mayor before, but I didn't think he'd made such a bold move until now. It left me feeling responsible, whether I was or not.

Hurst shook his head. "I don't think it was you. It's been building for weeks. Get your people safe."

"Thanks." Absolem clapped him on the shoulder.

March. Jo. Eliza. Everyone... Would we get there

in time? And even if we did, then what? The sheriff made it sound like we didn't have enough time to evacuate the clubhouse. What was going to happen to all of us tonight?

I hadn't made it this far, finally had hope for a future with March, only for it to end like this.

We were out of the precinct in a heartbeat, tearing through the night toward the club. The wind bit at my cheeks as we roared down the streets of town, but I barely noticed. My thoughts were consumed by the danger that awaited us.

"Call March," Absolem roared over the wind. "Warn him."

My fingers trembled as I dialed the number, praying he would answer. Praying we weren't too late. The call connected, and his voice filled my ears, rough with concern. "Vi?"

"We're coming," was all I could say before my voice broke. "Davis knows, March. The sheriff thinks he knows everything."

There was a brief silence, then a low curse. "Get here fast."

Absolem pushed the bike faster, the world streaking past in a blur of neon and darkness. Every second felt like an eternity, our impending confrontation with Davis looming large in front of us.

The club came into view, lights burning bright against the black night. We skidded to a halt in front of the entrance, leaping from the bike and rushing inside.

March was already there, rallying club members and preparing for a fight. His eyes met mine across the room -- the promise of what could have been reflected in his gaze -- but there was no time for sweet goodbyes or longing looks.

Murmurs echoed around us as Absolem revealed

Hurst's warning to the rest of the club. Determination hardened their features -- a fierce family ready to protect their own against any threat.

"We don't know when they're coming," Absolem finished his precipitous report. "But we need to be prepared."

"Then let's get ready," March growled.

Our preparations were frantic but methodical -- weapons checked, positions determined, a plan hastily put together. I was given a gun, the cold weight of it unfamiliar and terrifying in my hands. I'd watched my brother at the shooting range enough times to know the basics, but I wasn't sure I could actually hit anything if I tried.

As we waited for the inevitable, I found myself next to Absolem, his blue eyes watching the entrance with an unwavering stare.

"You ready?" he murmured.

"No," I admitted, my voice trembling with fear. "But I have to be."

"You're stronger than you realize," he said softly. "We'll face this together. Or you can hide with Jo and Eliza."

And for a moment, despite the impending danger outside our doors, I managed to believe him. "No. I'm going to fight."

The quiet was shattered by the roar of engines approaching. A chill ran down my spine -- the fight had arrived. We braced ourselves as headlights washed over the building, and Davis's men descended upon us.

The first shots rang out into the night air as we opened fire on the intruders. Fear surged within me -- I had never been in a real firefight. It was nothing like I'd seen on TV, and I realized I could very well die here. So could March.

Still, I held firm alongside my newfound family. March was front and center, his fierce gaze trained on the enemies before us. And so it began, our final stand against Mayor Davis.

I could only hope the club would come out on top and we wouldn't lose anyone.

If only I'd found the information faster... maybe we could have avoided this. But no amount of what-ifs were going to get us out of this.

* * *

March

I couldn't stop to focus on what was going on with Violet. I had to trust that she'd be okay. Part of me wished she'd have gone to hide with Jo and Eliza, but I knew that wasn't who she was. After the hell she'd been through, she wanted to stand up and fight.

I took down two more of the mayor's men with headshots before moving on to another one. Almost as soon as the fight started, it was over. Scanning the room, I took in the damage. Bullet holes riddled the walls. The windows had been shot out -- again. Mock had blood running down his arms, but it hadn't seemed to slow him down. Tweedle looked to have been shot in the thigh and I saw blood along his side. Knave, however, looked the worst of us all. He slumped against the wall, his breathing ragged.

Moving to his side, I checked him over. "Talk to me."

"Through and through in the shoulder. But there's one in my gut."

I winced. A gut shot was never a good thing. I lifted the hem of his shirt and checked the wound. It looked jagged and ugly. He'd need surgery for sure.

The blood on his side was just from a crease.

"Sheriff is on his way," Absolem said. "And your woman is fine. Shaken, but in one piece."

I nodded. As much as I wanted to rush to her side, I knew I had responsibilities to handle first. I was the Sergeant-at-Arms, and I needed to make sure my brothers and the women were safe. Not just *my* woman.

Even though Absolem had medical training, I still felt like this was my responsibility. To some degree, we all knew how to patch up wounds.

When the sheriff arrived, I let Hatter take the lead. An ambulance pulled up and they did what they could for Knave before loading him up. The rest of us would either patch ourselves up or go into the ER on our own. Knave was the only one who needed assistance to get there.

Once the chaos settled, I found Violet in the kitchen with the other women. She clutched Luna in her arms, and the kitten seemed content enough. Although, my presence made the little furball's eyes go wide, and it briefly tensed. The gunfire probably scared the shit out of the little thing.

"All of you all right?" I asked.

"We're good," Jo said. "How's Knave?"

"He should pull through. Won't know until a surgeon looks at hm. Bullet is still inside."

"And Mock?" Eliza asked.

I thought about the blood I'd noticed on his thigh. "I'm not sure. He either refused to ride in an ambulance, or it's not serious."

I kissed the top of Violet's head and breathed her in before leaving the kitchen. I still had work to do. Once the club was taken care of, then I'd go to the bedroom with her. If there was ever a night I needed to fall asleep with her in my arms, this was it. I only hoped she felt the same.

With my luck, I'd lose out to the damn cat.

Chapter Eight
Violet

The clubhouse's backyard was shrouded in darkness, save for the dim glow of a single bulb above the back door. Gravel crunched beneath our boots, the sound sharp in the silence.

I turned to him, my heart hammering. His blue eyes locked onto mine, reflecting a storm of emotions that mirrored my own. Without a word, he stepped closer, the heat from his body radiating against the chill of the air.

His hands found my waist, pulling me into him. The world narrowed down to the touch of his calloused fingers through the thin fabric of my shirt, the warmth of his breath on my skin.

His lips crashed onto mine, insistent and demanding. The kiss ignited something fierce and desperate, a fire that consumed all thought. I melted against him, tangling my fingers in the short hair at the nape of his neck, surrendering to the onslaught of sensation.

But as quickly as the blaze had erupted, it was smothered. March pulled away, leaving me gasping for air, my lips tingling from the loss of contact.

"Shit," he muttered under his breath, his jaw clenched tight. The guilt that shadowed his features was unmistakable. Ben -- my brother, his best friend -- loomed between us once more. I'd thought we'd moved past this last night, but apparently not. Or maybe, despite how much he said he wanted me or needed me, some part of him felt like he was betraying his friendship with my brother? I wouldn't know if I didn't ask.

"March?" I reached for him, my chest

constricting with a mix of confusion and fear. "What's wrong?"

He shook his head, the lines of his face hardening. "This... us... It's not simple, Vi."

"Nothing about life is simple," I replied, my breath forming clouds in the cold air. I could feel the weight of his internal battle, the struggle between desire and duty. "It's not supposed to be. Living is messy, painful, but it can also be beautiful. Those beautiful moments are what make the rest of it worthwhile."

"Ben wouldn't have wanted --" He stopped himself, the sentence hanging unfinished, heavy with implication.

"Ben's gone, March." The words were a knife in my own heart, but they needed to be said. "We can't keep living for a ghost. And I'm not sure my brother would have disapproved. He knew you better than anyone. If he was ever going to trust someone not to break my heart, it would be you."

He looked at me then, really looked, and I saw it -- the flicker of resolve behind his eyes. But it was the pain, raw and unfiltered, that held my gaze. Pain for the past we'd lost, for the future we were uncertain how to claim.

"Violet..." His hand lifted, brushing a stray lock of hair from my face with a tenderness that belied his rugged exterior.

I leaned into his touch, willing him to understand that some risks were worth taking. That even in the chaos of our world, there was a chance for something real.

"Let's not think about tomorrow, just tonight," I said softly, daring to close the space between us once more. "We can take things one day at a time."

I stepped back, the cold biting through my clothes as I put distance between us. March's eyes were a storm of blue, churning with conflict and something deeper, something that sent shivers down my spine that weren't from the chill in the air.

"Do you regret this? Us?"

He remained silent for a heartbeat too long, and I felt a pang of fear that maybe he did. Maybe we were just two lost souls colliding in the night, destined to crash and burn. But then he moved, his hand reaching out, slow but steady.

He took my hand, his grip strong and warm. "I don't regret a single damn thing."

The sincerity in his eyes pinned me in place. His touch seared into me, branding his promise onto my skin. And just like that, the world shifted beneath us, our connection solidifying into something unshakeable. Even if Ben came between us again, I knew we'd get past it, just like we had now. Nothing in life worth having was ever easy, and that was doubly true of relationships.

The air between us, once heavy with unspoken fears, now felt alive with possibility. My heart hammered against my ribs as I leaned in, pressing my lips to his with renewed conviction. This kiss wasn't just about seeking comfort -- it was a declaration. I was his and he was mine.

His response was immediate, powerful. March's arms enveloped me, pulling me into the fortress of his embrace. His touch was a shield, his body a barrier against the chaos of the world outside our secluded haven.

"I swear on everything I am -- I'll keep you safe."

In the cocoon of his arms, I allowed myself to believe in the sanctuary we could create together.

Other than the one incident, things had been quiet here. It made me wonder if we'd have lots of days like this, or if my past would come back to haunt me. It didn't seem like those men were looking for me. Even if they were, how would they find me? Now that I was here, now that I had March back in my life, things would be okay.

The pulse of his heart thrummed against my cheek, a steadfast drum in the stillness of the night. His arms, my sanctuary, tightened just enough to remind me I wasn't alone.

"March," I whispered, the courage surging like adrenaline through my veins. "I'm scared."

His embrace didn't falter. It was the rock in a raging sea. "Talk to me."

My breath hitched as I pulled back, looking up into eyes that had seen so much yet still managed to hold such gentleness for me. My hand instinctively rested on my still flat belly in a protective gesture. "It's not just us anymore."

He listened, his gaze never leaving mine. The dim light from the clubhouse windows cast stark shadows across his face, accentuating the lines of concern etched there. But he stayed silent, giving me the space to voice the fears that gnawed at my soul.

"Violence... retaliation... It's part of the world you live in. Part of the world we live in now. What if -- " I swallowed hard. "When the mayor sent those men here, I could have died. *You* could have. Does a baby even stand a chance?"

He took my hands in his, grounding me. "We'll face it all. Together."

"Can we really protect our baby from --"

"From anything and everything," he assured me, his conviction sharp as steel. "You have my word.

You'll never be alone in this. You have me and everyone else here. The kid is going to have a bunch of overprotective uncles."

His words reassured me, even though the fear didn't completely dissipate. I wasn't sure it ever would. At least, not until this town felt completely safe.

* * *

March

Life at the clubhouse wasn't always peaceful. With the place filled with mostly single men, there was a party more often than not. Although, not quite as much as since Jo and Eliza had joined us. At least, not the same types. Even then, it wasn't like we'd been wild. Not like some of the clubs I'd met. Tonight, music had been blasting from the speakers in the common room before it had even gotten dark outside.

The night had turned ink-black by the time we decided to retreat from the solitude of the clubhouse's shadowy backyard. Violet's hand in mine was a lifeline, her skin warm against the cool evening air. We moved together, almost as if we'd been doing it all our lives.

Our room became our sanctuary, the door shutting out the world. And yes, I was starting to think of this as *our* space. She still hadn't moved out of the guest room, but I had a feeling it was only a matter of time.

Clothes fell away, and we tumbled to the bed, getting tangled in the sheets. I felt desperate for her, hungry. The way she kissed me back said she felt the same.

I pulled her closer, my hands exploring every inch of her soft skin. She moaned, arching into my touch, her nipples hardening against my chest. We rolled over, and Vi spread her legs invitingly, revealing her glistening pink pussy.

I kissed my way down her stomach, not stopping until my shoulders pressed her thighs wider apart. "You're so fucking beautiful."

I pushed my tongue inside her, tasting her sweetness. She gasped, her hips bucking off the bed. I pulled away, leaning back to stare at the perfection laid out before me. She watched me intently, her eyes filled with trust and submission.

"Are you ready for me?" I asked.

She nodded shakily. "Please."

Coming up over her, I wedged my hips between her thighs. She welcomed me inside, her legs wrapping around my waist. I slid in easily, nearly groaning at how amazing she felt. We moved together in a coordinated rhythm, our breaths coming in ragged gasps. She arched her back, pushing her breasts out, begging for more.

I reached between us, rubbing her little clit, and thrust into her again and again. She screamed in pleasure. I didn't stop, didn't slow. I took her like a man possessed, and maybe I was.

"You like that?" I asked, my voice rough.

"Yes." She whimpered. "Please, don't stop."

I pulled all the way out and plunged back in, harder this time, hitting that sweet spot inside her. She cried out, her nails digging into my back. I reached down, pinching her nipple, eliciting another moan.

I picked up speed, pounding into her with unrelenting force. She met every thrust, panting and writhing beneath me. I couldn't hold back anymore. My cock throbbed with need. With one last hard thrust, I came inside her, my whole body shuddering with release.

We lay there panting, our hearts racing.

"That was amazing," she whispered. "I've never felt anything like that before. Even last time... Well, this was just different."

I smiled, knowing this was only the beginning.

I helped her out of bed, and we cleaned up together in the shower before lying down once more. It didn't take long for her to fall asleep in my arms. But peace didn't claim her. Instead, tortured whispers slipped from her lips -- names that knifed through the quiet, had me focused on what she was saying. Michael Wright. Tyler Murray. The ghosts of her past demanding attention.

I disentangled myself gently. Pulling on my jeans, I made my way through the clubhouse, searching for the only other hacker I knew. Absolem was outside, alone, smoke curling around his solemn face. My approach was silent, but his eyes flicked to me, recognizing the urgency before I spoke.

"I've got two names: Michael Wright, Tyler Murray. Dig up everything. It's priority. I think they're in my hometown."

His nod was curt, blue eyes steeling over. "Consider it done, March. They won't hide long."

He didn't even ask why I wanted to know. Bastard probably already knew. It didn't take a genius to figure out what would pull me from bed when I had a naked woman in my arms.

"Thanks," I muttered, clapping a hand on his shoulder before retreating back into our makeshift haven, where nightmares dared to tread. Violet's nightmare was now mine to wage war against. And I'd spill blood for justice, no matter the cost.

Returning inside, I found Violet stirring, her eyelashes fluttering open. She searched my face for something -- reassurance, perhaps.

"Hey," I whispered, slipping beside her, enveloping her in an embrace that sought to banish the shadows from her eyes. "You okay?"

Her lips curved into a brave smile, one that fought back the remnants of her nightmare. "Better than fine," she murmured.

I held her a little longer before urging her from the bed. We dressed in silence, the fabric of our clothes whispering over skin still warm from each other's touch.

Together, we stepped into the common room where the rest of the club moved about, oblivious to the tempest brewing beneath my calm surface. Violet squeezed my hand, and I squeezed back.

I didn't know what we were celebrating tonight, but it seemed everyone was still going strong. The thump of bass pulsed through the clubhouse walls. Violet released my hand, and I watched as she moved among the brothers, her dark hair catching glints of light. Despite the horrors that had chased her into sleep, she seemed fine now.

She turned, those whiskey eyes finding mine, and there was a spark there. She waited as I caught up to her, my hand finding hers.

"Let's dance," I suggested. It wasn't something I'd particularly enjoyed, but I knew Vi did, and I'd do anything for her. Even make a fool of myself in front of everyone here.

Violet nodded, a smile playing on her lips. She fit perfectly against me as we swayed to the beat, her curves molded to my frame. Her head rested against my chest. This moment, this connection, it was what I fought for -- what I would die for.

"Feel that?" I whispered, my mouth close to her

ear.

"Your heart," she murmured back.

"Yeah." My arms tightened around her. "Beating for you."

"Mine's yours," she confessed.

The world narrowed down to the space between us, the shared warmth of our bodies, and the promise of tomorrow. As we danced, I felt the weight of the past and the pull of the future. With Violet in my arms, I knew one thing for certain -- we weren't just surviving.

We were living.

The night wrapped around us as I lowered my head to hers. I kissed her like my life depended on it, not caring if my brothers saw. They'd give me shit later, but right now, I needed to prove to both myself and her that she was mine. Violet melted against me, and I held her tight, never wanting the moment to end.

In her, I'd found a reason to keep going, to forgive myself. There wasn't anything I wouldn't do for her.

Chapter Nine
March

The room was still dark, the soft glow of dawn just a promise behind closed curtains. We lay there, tangled in sweat-dampened sheets, the echo of our cries still hanging in the air. My fingers danced lightly over Violet's skin, drawing aimless patterns along her spine. I could feel the rise and fall of her breath, slow and steady, but I wanted to memorize every curve and hollow of her body.

"Marcus," she whispered. She stirred beside me, her body a portrait of vulnerability etched into the mattress. Her eyes fluttered open and I saw it. The shadow of a nightmare lurking in their depths. She hadn't been vocal with this one. If I wasn't looking at her right now, I'd have never known she had one. How many nights had she suffered in silence?

She shifted closer, seeking the warmth of my skin against hers -- a silent plea for comfort, for the assurance that the horrors of her mind couldn't reach her here.

"Bad dream?" I asked, even though I knew the answer. I felt the slight nod against my chest, her hair brushing my skin. My arms tightened around her involuntarily, the protector in me roaring silently against anything that dared threaten her peace.

"You're safe now," I assured her. Nothing would touch her -- not the shadows of the past nor the dangers that prowled beyond our doors. I'd do whatever it took to keep her safe.

She exhaled, a long, shuddering breath that seemed to release the last vestiges of her unease. "I know."

I kissed her forehead softly. In the quiet that

followed, I held her close, the steady beat of her heart syncing with mine. There was no need for more words. I remained awake, watching over her as she slept a few more hours. Light began to filter into the room, and I knew another day had started. I felt the tension in her before she fully woke.

She blinked, her eyes focusing slowly. Her body melded against mine, a perfect fit. I didn't like thinking about the years we'd lost, time we could have been together if I hadn't been running.

"Want to talk about your dream last night?" I asked.

Her breath hitched. "There were guns... and blood. They wouldn't stop chasing me. It felt so real."

"Shh," I hushed her gently. "It's over now."

I'd stand as her shield against the darkness that wanted to swallow her whole. She wouldn't face it alone -- not now, not ever.

"It's like I can't escape," she murmured. "I think that's what bothers me. They let me go. Why? I saw their faces. What if they'd planned to come back, but I ran? Will they track me down? The not knowing was bothering me. I was terrified every day, constantly looking over my shoulder. The only thing I could think of that would make me feel safe was you."

"If they do, then I'll take them down. Every last one." I wasn't going to confess I had Absolem looking into two of them already. I'd handle it quietly, assuming he could track them down. It wasn't like I'd given him a lot to go on. I'd assumed they were from my hometown, and the two names she'd mentioned were common enough. But I had to hope Absolem could piece it all together, since Vi didn't seem too keen on discussing it in detail.

I leaned in, my lips finding the warmth of her

forehead. The act was simple but heavy with all the unsaid things between us. Love. Loyalty. And something deeper. She'd been a part of my life for as long as I could remember. I'd never once considered how her role might change over time, but now that I had her here in my arms, I wasn't planning to ever let go.

My lips sought hers. It wasn't just a touch. I did my best to brand myself onto her soul, lay claim to everything she was, and gave just as much of myself back.

Her arms wrapped around my neck, pulling me closer. The urgency of her touch ignited something primal within me, a surge of desire that demanded I mark every inch of her as mine.

"You won't ever let me go, right?" she asked.

"Never," I vowed, sealing it with another kiss. Until her, I'd never felt like I was part of someone, incomplete without them. Violet was special to me in every way possible. I only hoped she realized it. I couldn't remember if I'd told her exactly how I felt. "I love you more than I thought possible."

Her gaze locked onto mine, tears shimmering, unshed but very much there. She blinked slowly and one tear escaped, rolling down her cheek. She didn't have to say the words back to me. I already knew how she felt.

"I've found peace here... with you. This is where I belong. I've always belonged by your side, and I think I knew that even when I was only eight years old."

My chest tightened as if a band of steel had wrapped around it. Her declaration, simple yet profound, cut through every layer of armor I'd ever worn.

I pulled the blanket over us, wanting to block out the world. Her fingers traced the lines of my tattoos, silent stories etched into my flesh. Each one a scar, a battle, a memory. But now, they were also a testament -- a map of survival that led to her.

Before I could even think of devouring her again, a soft meow drew my attention to the foot of the bed. Luna still stayed in the footlocker, but soon, I'd have to release her and let her roam the room. The day after I'd found her, I'd had a bag of kitten food delivered to the clubhouse, along with a dish. So far, she'd been good about using the litter box.

"Your furry child wants your attention," Violet said, and I felt the curve of her lips against me as she smiled.

I placed my hand over her belly. "How many months until a human baby is crying for us?"

She went still beside me, and I realized I'd pretty much just claimed her kid as mine. She'd referred to it as "our" baby, but it was the first time I'd said as much. Truthfully, I'd decided almost from the start I'd be a dad to this baby. Without Ben, Violet didn't have other men to rely on. It's why she'd come to find me to begin with.

"Are you really ready to accept this baby as yours?" she asked.

"Didn't realize that was even a question." I leaned up on my elbow to look down at her. "You came here asking for help, for protection. Did you think I'd let you stay and tell you to get rid of the kid?"

She shook her head. "No, I guess I just…"

"What?"

"I'd hoped you might want to be part of my baby's life, but I was too scared to believe it could ever really happen. Of course, I'd also thought you'd never see me as more than Ben's little sister."

"People change, Vi. I'm not the same man you used to know. For one, I was still a kid back then. We haven't seen each other much since I enlisted, and not all the last few years."

She narrowed her eyes at me. "And whose fault is that?"

"Very much mine, and I'm sorry."

The kitten cried again, and I got up to check on her. Luna had drunk all her water so I got her more and topped off her food. After giving her a scratch behind the ear, I sat on the edge of the bed. Before I could open my mouth and say anything, someone banged on the bedroom door.

"Hatter needs everyone in the common room. Women too," Mock yelled through the door.

I helped Vi out of bed and we both quickly dressed before joining everyone else. I sat at the table with Jo, Eliza, and Cheshire, pulling Violet down onto my lap. She leaned against me, and we focused on the club president.

"First off, Knave is coming home later. He'll have to take it easy for a bit, but he's going to be fine." Several people clapped and whistled, so Hatter waited for it to be quiet again. "And I have news about the mayor and Robert Lewis. Both men are in custody. The information we gave Sheriff Hurst, in addition to the mayor trying to have our club taken out, gave law enforcement everything they needed to lock those two up."

"What about the girls?" Violet asked.

"Park said the FBI would be looking into it. The ones shipped overseas are likely out of reach, assuming they're still alive. But our part in all this is finished. I don't want you or Absolem digging anymore. Right now the FBI is looking the other way, but if you hack into any other government files, they may not be so nice about it."

Violet nodded. "Understood."

"So the town is now safe?" Jo asked. "It's all over?"

"Park has done his best to weed out all the bad deputies, and I'm sure there may be a few bad apples still in the mayor's office, but for the most part… yes."

"What do we do now?" Tweedle asked. "We haven't had a moment's peace in a while. Not sure I know what to do with myself without an enemy to focus on."

Hatter smiled. "Yeah, but it's a problem I don't mind solving. I thought we could do a few things, actually."

"Like?" Cheshire prompted.

"Open a business in town. Maybe two. In addition to that, I want to help this community."

I knew why we hadn't made a move before now. We'd helped in small ways where we could, but we'd been so focused on gaining the town's support, then weeding out the corrupt officials, none of us had had the time to dedicate to getting a business off the ground. Looked like the club was ready to take that leap now.

"We aren't your typical club," he continued. "I'm well aware of that. Doesn't mean we can't reach out to some other MCs and see if they'd be interested in a charity ride with all the proceeds going to help the shelter Sister Mary is running."

"I can get behind that," I said. "As long as we aren't asking one percent clubs to join in. Not sure I want them around our women."

Hatter arched an eyebrow. "Some of them aren't

any worse than we are, or need I remind you what happened to the dearly departed sheriff?"

I shrugged. If he found guys who were good and just did bad things for all the right reasons, then I wouldn't have an issue with it. Might be nice to get more connections. There had to be other clubs out there with veterans too. It would be good to meet more men and women who'd come home and found the same solution to retaining a brotherhood, or sisterhood.

"There's one more order of business. Our club is growing. Even though we aren't accepting prospects or new members, we all seem to be starting families. Pretty soon this clubhouse won't hold us all. I haven't come up with a solution just yet, but I'm open to ideas." Hatter waved us off. "Now, go back to whatever you were doing. That's all I've got for now."

Hatter came over and Jo stood. Once he'd sat down, she claimed his lap. Three of the club officers now had women and babies on the way. It made me wonder who might fall next. Rabbit? Tweedle? Absolem? I didn't see it being Mock, Knave, or Carpenter. The first two enjoyed women too much, and Carpenter... well, I wasn't sure what to think of him some days.

"Does this mean we can move about town freely now?" Eliza asked. "Because I'm a little tired of constantly needing a shadow."

Cheshire smacked her on the thigh. "Wishful thinking. If you believe for one second I'm letting you leave this place without a guard, you're crazier than I thought."

"Dad is gone, and now so are the mayor and Mr. Lewis," she said. "So why can't I?"

Cheshire stared at her for a long moment. "I

thought I would die when you disappeared before and I had no idea where you were. The monsters we know about are gone. Doesn't mean there isn't still evil here. I can't go through that again, Eliza. Don't ask me to."

It was the most serious I'd seen him in a long time. Well, except during a battle. But I got it. I'd feel the same if Violet suddenly vanished. I'd probably lose my shit and want to tear the world apart in an attempt to find her.

"When are you going to let the kitten run free?" Jo asked. "I want to play with it."

I raised an eyebrow at her sudden change of topic, but I saw the pleading look in her eyes and relented. "Not anytime soon. It's so damn small I think I may lose it in the bedroom. Doesn't mean you can't come see her."

"Can we get a cat?" Eliza asked, looking over at Cheshire.

He grinned and pointed to his face. "You already have one. A most superb species too."

She rolled her eyes, and I had to cough to cover my laughter. Something told me, sooner or later, Cheshire would be welcoming a cat into his life. Because if Eliza really wanted one, he wouldn't tell her no. Not for long anyway.

Was this what peace felt like? Would things become more laid back and normal now?

I had to say it didn't totally suck.

Chapter Ten
Violet

"Hop on," March said, patting the seat behind him.

I hesitated. I'd enjoyed our last ride, even if it had been a bit scary at first. But I had a life growing inside me. Was it safe to keep riding with him like this? He revved the engine, and my feet carried me over to him, almost as if on their own. I swung my leg over the seat and settled behind him, placing my feet where he'd shown me before, and putting my hands on his waist.

"Wrap your arms around me," March instructed, his tone leaving no room for argument.

I slid my arms around his waist, feeling the hard planes of his stomach beneath my fingers. His scent enveloped me, and I breathed him in.

"Ready?" His voice was almost gentle now, a stark contrast to the usual authority it carried.

"Ready."

He chuckled softly. I clutched at him tighter, my nails digging into the leather of his cut, as he eased toward the driveway.

"Remember, hold on tight," he said.

And then we picked up speed and took off, the clubhouse disappearing behind us as the motorcycle devoured the road beneath its wheels. I pressed my face into his back, allowing his presence to shelter me from the onslaught of speed and sound.

"Never let go, Vi," he shouted back at me, and I could only nod against him, my world reduced to the thunderous heartbeat of the motorcycle and the man who commanded it.

The world stretched infinitely, a canvas of black

asphalt and lingering twilight. March leaned into every curve, the bike an extension of his own steely will. Wind clawed at my hair, tugging it free from any semblance of order. I tightened my grip on him, the solid certainty of his presence anchoring me.

"Keep your eyes open, Vi," he yelled over the roar of the engine. "You don't want to miss anything."

I forced my eyes open as the landscape blurred into streaks of darkening colors, smudges of green and brown that fought against the encroaching night. My breath came in short bursts, the air crisp and biting as it filled my lungs. Exhilaration filled me, spreading warmth. I found myself leaning with March, embracing the rhythm of the ride.

"Good, Violet," March's approval cut through the rushing wind. "Feel it, don't fight it. Lean with the bike."

My heart hammered, not in dread now, but in wild abandon. The countryside flew past us, a painting in motion, and I was part of it. Each breath I took was laced with the scent of earth and adrenaline, a heady mix that set my senses alight.

March glanced back at me, a glint of something fierce and proud in his blue eyes. In that moment, as the bike ate up the miles beneath us, I realized I was soaring. Not just clinging to March but flying beside him through the dusk.

The road curved, a serpentine path that snaked through an ocean of rolling hills and lush meadows. March's grip on the throttle was steady, confidence radiating from him. He navigated each bend with precision, a master of motion and momentum. I clung to him, thrilling in every twist and turn.

I dared to lift my gaze, and the landscapes unfurled like pages in a storybook. Hills dipped and rose, with mountain peaks as a backdrop. The sun ignited the horizon in flames of orange and red. Trees stood as sentinels along our route, their leaves whispering secrets long forgotten.

We were poetry in motion, the motorcycle and us, a symphony of growling engine and whistling wind. A hunger filled me for the unknown stretches of road ahead.

"It's beautiful!" I yelled over the wind.

"Nothing compared to you," he shouted back, the words almost lost but not quite. They reached me and wrapped around my soul like a promise.

Each sharp turn we took was a dance, and I was learning the steps -- one beat of exhilaration at a time. We leaned into the curves, a perfect balance of danger and control. The motorcycle's tires kissed the asphalt like a lover's embrace.

Freedom. It coursed through me, a potent drug that filled my veins with liquid fire. With March, I tasted life raw and unfiltered. The world stretched out before us, vast and untamed, and I wanted to devour it whole.

"Never stop," I said as close to his ear as possible, wanting to be heard over the wind. "I want to ride forever."

"We'll ride whenever you want to."

We charged forward, two hearts racing in tandem, chasing the fading light as it retreated into the embrace of dusk. And in that chase, I found something I never knew I'd lost -- a piece of myself.

The engine's growl softened. March was easing off the throttle. I glanced up, catching his eyes in the sideview mirror. That small smile of his played on his lips again. I loved this side of him.

"Enjoying yourself?" he asked.

"More than I thought possible," I admitted.

"Good."

We banked a gentle curve, and there it was -- a vista so vast it stole my breath. March pulled over, the motorcycle coming to a rest with a final purr. The world around us stood still for just a moment, holding its breath along with mine.

"Wow." My whisper felt sacrilegious in the face of such beauty.

"Come on." He swung his leg over the bike, gesturing for me to join him.

I dismounted, boots crunching on gravel, and followed March's lead to where the earth fell away into eternity. The view stretched out endlessly before us, a tapestry of greens and golds woven together by an unseen artist's hand.

"Beautiful," I murmured.

The world was quieter here. I took a deep breath, letting the cool air fill my lungs and steady my nerves.

"Come on." March's voice was soft but insistent.

I moved forward, drawn inexorably toward the precipice. The edge of the cliff beckoned like a promise, the drop beyond it a whisper of danger. The land below sprawled out in a riot of color, rolling hills undulating in the afternoon sun. Fields of green clashed against patches of earthy brown, the natural palette vibrant and alive.

March's presence was solid beside me, an anchor in the fluid landscape. He stood close enough for his warmth to seep into me. His gaze, usually so piercing, now softened as he surveyed the horizon, the lines of his face relaxing into something almost serene.

"Never gets old," he murmured, his words floating away on the wind. "I like to come here when it feels like the walls are closing in on me."

The beauty of the scene was stark, almost brutal in its splendor. It was a life of contrasts, where moments of peace were hard-won and all the more precious for it. Which made me cherish this moment even more.

We stood silently together, just admiring the scenery. There was no need for words. The view said everything that needed to be said. We were just two people enjoying a rare moment of tranquility in the embrace of nature's grand design.

I turned to March, my breath catching at the raw intensity in his blue eyes, reflecting the dying light. This man turned me inside out. He made me feel so many things, and with an intensity that scared me sometimes.

"Thank you," I whispered, the words barely escaping before he closed the distance between us.

His lips met mine with a force that spoke volumes, more than we could ever say aloud. The kiss wasn't just a meeting of mouths. It was an exchange of silent promises and unspoken understandings. My arms instinctively wrapped tighter around him, clinging to the man who had become my unexpected haven in a world that had shown me too much darkness.

I felt his fingers trail along my jaw, grounding me to the moment. Our connection crackled like the air before a storm, electric and unstoppable. Reluctantly, we parted. The sun dipped lower, streaking the sky with orange and purple hues, a fiery backdrop to our silhouette.

"Time to go," March said, his voice rough, edged with the same reluctance that mirrored mine.

"Yeah." The word was merely a whisper.

We moved toward the bike, my legs still shaky

from the ride and the emotions that coursed through us. Mounting the motorcycle once again, the leather seat felt different now, almost welcoming. I settled behind him, wrapping my arms around his waist with a newfound sense of belonging.

The engine roared to life beneath us, a beast awakened, and with one final glance at the horizon, we surged forward. The clubhouse awaited our return. I carried with me the afterglow of the sunset and the heat of March's kiss, embers of a fire that promised to burn long into the night. I wondered if we'd spend another night wrapped in each other's arms.

March's body was a solid presence in front of me. I clung to him, the rumble of the engine a steady thrum between my thighs.

Trees blurred into shadows as we raced past, their branches reaching out like fingers trying to snatch at the last light of day. The wind was colder now, the warmth of the sun a mere memory against our skin. But inside, a heat lingered, stoked by March's unwavering strength and the intensity of his kiss.

He leaned into a curve, the bike tilting, but his control was absolute. This man, with his scars and his solemn eyes, held my safety in his hands as deftly as he handled the machine under us. Lights flickered in the distance, and March's posture shifted, signaling that our ride was coming to a close.

The motorcycle slowed, its growl subsiding to a purr as we approached the entrance. He brought it to a halt, the silence of the engine magnifying the sudden stillness around us.

"Here we are," March said, his voice low and gravelly, slicing through the quiet.

"Back to reality," I replied, unwilling to let go of the freedom the ride had given me.

March turned slightly, his blue eyes catching the faint light. "Not all of it has to end."

His words brought back our kiss, and my cheeks warmed. It looked like we'd be spending another night with me screaming his name and him sending me to new heights. I wasn't going to complain. I craved March like a drug.

My legs trembled as I slid off the bike. March's hands were on my waist in an instant, steadying me.

"Got you," he murmured.

"Thanks." My heart raced, not from the ride but from him, from us.

We locked eyes for a moment, something unspoken passing between us. Then, hand in hand, we turned toward the clubhouse. His grip was firm, reassuring.

As our boots crunched on the gravel, I couldn't help but feel a sense of calm that was in stark contrast to the chaos within those walls. But outside with March by my side, I felt protected from that noise. In this moment, I wasn't just trying to survive. I was truly living and enjoying life.

"Feels different, doesn't it?" I asked.

"Everything does now," he replied, his thumb tracing circles on the back of my hand -- a sensation that sent sparks up my arm. "Ready?"

"Always," I answered. Together, we stepped over the threshold, into our home.

I'd found the place where I belonged. Being here with March brought new meaning to my life. He was my everything, and I had no idea how I'd survived without him all this time.

The sound of laughter and music greeted us as we walked in, but it was just white noise. My attention was solely on March, the man who had shown me a world I never knew existed. A world where I could be myself without fear of judgment.

We made it to our room, and he pulled me into his arms again. He kissed me, and I melted into him, surrendering under his touch. His hands roamed my body with ownership yet tenderness.

"I want to savor every moment with you," he murmured.

"We have a lifetime together, Marcus. I'm not going anywhere."

"No." He leaned in to kiss me softly. "You're not. If you even tried to leave, I'd find you. I won't ever let you go, Vi. Not now, not ever."

"I'd never run from you. *To* you, but not from you." I reached up to cup his cheek. "This is what I've wanted for so very long. Now that I'm yours, and you're mine, I have everything I need."

"Same, Vi. I feel the very same."

Chapter Eleven
March

The roar of voices and the clink of beer bottles filled the club's air. The mayor and Robert Lewis mess was over, and Knave was back home. Needless to say, my brothers were eager to shift focus. Plans for runs, community rides, charity events -- they were all laid out.

"All right, let's button this up. Next order --"

I interrupted Hatter, as I stood abruptly. Scanning the room, I realized not only was Violet *not* beside me, but I didn't see her anywhere in the room. "Where's Vi?"

She should've been here, by my side where it was safe. My gut twisted, instinct telling me something was off. No matter where I looked, she wasn't here. This didn't seem like something she'd want to miss. Had she just gone back to our room?

"Damn it," I muttered under my breath. "Spread out. Check every corner of this place."

My brothers scattered, everyone looking for Violet. She wasn't in the community bathroom. Kitchen was empty. Same for our room. Someone checked the garage and out back of the clubhouse. "Someone get on the phone, call her cell. Now!"

They knew what Vi meant to me, to us -- she was family, and the Underland MC protected its own. I'd go through our room again. Maybe she'd left a note and just stepped out? But that didn't seem likely.

"Check the parking lot. Anywhere she might've stepped out for air," I ordered, pushing through the throng, my heart slamming against my ribs.

I went to our bedroom and searched the space. I didn't see anything out of place. Same for the rest of the clubhouse. I eyed the back door. Had someone been brave enough to slip inside here and snatch her out from under our noses? I knew our security needed to be beefed up, but it was easier said than done. It would take time and a lot of money. But after this, I'd make damn sure every fucking exterior door in this place had a camera watching it.

One after another, they all reported back. No one could find her. What the hell? I'd been in a meeting with Cheshire and Hatter before we'd called in the rest of the club. How had I not realized she was missing before now? I'd just assumed she'd be with Jo and Eliza. The three of them had gotten close rather quickly. It wasn't until I found them in the crowd I realized Vi wasn't with them, and she sure the fuck hadn't been beside me.

"Find her," I said. My voice was steady, even though I felt like I might erupt at any moment. Every second she was missing, the danger multiplied. Every moment of uncertainty was a knife-edge against my throat. Who the hell could have taken her? Had the sheriff's department missed someone aligned with the mayor? Had they taken Violet for revenge? Or did it not have to do with that at all?

"Anything? Any sign?" I pressed, watching as heads shook, frustration mounting.

"Her car's still here," someone called out from the doorway, a sliver of information that was both reassuring and terrifying. She hadn't left willingly. No way she'd have gone far on foot.

"Keep looking!" I barked, my muscles coiled, ready to tear apart the earth to find her. Fear clawed at me, a feral thing, but I stamped it down. There was no room for fear, not when Vi needed me.

"March, we'll find her," Tweedle said, his hand

on my shoulder.

"Move faster!" I snarled, already dialing contacts who owed me favors, anyone who could give me a lead. "She's out there somewhere, scared and alone..."

No way Violet would have left without a word. No, the only conclusion I could come to was that she'd been taken. I had no idea who would do such a thing. Unless... She'd been worried about the men who had hurt her. Could they have possibly tracked her here? For what purpose?

I wouldn't rest until Violet was back, safe within the walls of the clubhouse, back within my reach where I could shield her from the world's cruelties.

"Vi," I whispered, a prayer tossed into the chaos. "Hang on. I'm coming for you."

I stormed through the clubhouse, my boots thudding against the floor. Heart pounding, I made a beeline for Absolem. He was our eyes and ears, the man who could find a ghost millions of miles away.

"Absolem!" My voice cut through the clamor of the main room, razor-sharp with urgency. He looked up, his eyes zeroing in on mine.

"Already got my computer," he said, motioning to the machine in front of him.

"Track her phone," I ordered, my words wrapped in steel. "Now."

"Already on it," he replied without missing a beat, fingers flying over the keyboard. The screens flickered with lines of code.

"Anything, you let me know. Immediately." There was no mistaking the command in my voice. I wasn't just looking for my other half. I was the club's Sergeant-at-Arms.

"Got it, March," he responded, his focus unbreakable as he delved into the virtual abyss searching for Vi.

Turning away, I surveyed the room -- my brothers, faces etched with concern and determination. One of our own was out there, alone, and every second counted.

"Listen up!" I bellowed, and the room fell silent. "We're splitting up. Informants, local hangouts, anyone who might've seen something, anything. I want boots on the ground, eyes everywhere."

"Mock, Carpenter, hit the bars and gas stations. Someone had to see something." They nodded, already grabbing their jackets.

"Rabbit start calling around. Anyone owes us favors, cash them in. We need information." My orders were terse, met with immediate action.

"Knave, since you're still out of commission, I want you here. Coordinate the search, keep everyone in line. You can handle that from a chair." His nod was solemn.

"Move, move, move!" The clubhouse erupted into activity.

"Find her," I whispered under my breath, a command to the universe. Fear nipped at my heels, but I couldn't let it take hold. Not when Vi needed me to be the rock she could cling to in the storm.

As they dispersed, I clenched my fists. Every second was a step closer to bringing her back to where she belonged -- with me, with us. I had to believe that.

"Stay strong, Vi," I murmured.

My phone rang and I pressed it to my ear as I answered. "Talk to me."

"I've got wind of something. A new player in town. Word is they snatched a girl," Mock said. "The clerk at the gas station said we could see their camera footage. I'm hoping we catch a break."

"If anything changes, you let me know." I ended the call, adrenaline surging through my veins. It wasn't a guaranteed lead, but it was more than I'd had moments ago.

Absolem growled and slammed his fist onto the table. "Damnit! Her phone is here. There has to be something else."

"She has one of those fancy watches. The kind that tracks your steps, monitors your heartbeat. Maybe it has a GPS?" Jo asked.

"On it," Absolem said.

Mock called back. He started talking the moment the line connected. "I can't tell for sure if this is our guy, but there's definitely someone shady and it seems like he has a woman in his car. Can't get a good look at her to know if it's Violet."

"Where did they go?" I asked.

"East side of town."

I sighed. "Get there now. Even if it's nothing, we need to check it out."

"Got a lead?" Cheshire asked.

"Yeah. East side of town. Mock is on his way there now."

"Go," Hatter said. "You won't rest until you know if it's her. I'll stay here with the women and Knave."

I gave him a brief nod before pulling my keys from my pocket. I hoped like hell it really was her. If not, then it meant we still had no fucking clue where she was or what happened to her.

* * *

Mock and I descended on the warehouse where he'd tracked down the man from the gas station footage. This place had seen better days, but tonight, it was an arena, and we were going to battle. We slipped through the darkness, clinging to the shadows.

I took point, pressing my back against the cold metal siding of the warehouse. Vi's face flashed in my mind -- her eyes haunted, pleading for rescue.

My hand closed around the handle of the door. It turned with a creak of protest, opening onto a void. The darkness inside felt alive, pulsing with unseen threats. I stepped into the abyss with Mock right on my heels. My eyes adjusted slowly, shapes emerging from the gloom -- pallets stacked high, chains dangling from the ceiling, shadows within shadows. A maze.

I crept forward, every sense straining. I moved deeper, navigating the labyrinth of crates and machinery. Every corner turned brought us closer to our goal, or so I hoped.

The warehouse seemed to tighten around us, a noose drawing closed. Each step felt heavier, each breath laced with the tang of impending violence. She was here, somewhere amidst the steel and stone. She had to be. I refused to accept any other truth.

"Vi," I whispered. "We're coming."

And we pushed deeper into the belly of the beast, ready to tear the world apart to bring one of our own back home, I started to think we'd entered an empty building. Then I saw it.

"Tripwire," I whispered, my hand shooting out to stop my brother in his tracks. His nod was tight, a silent thanks as we stepped over the gleaming wire, barely visible against the concrete floor.

We moved like ghosts. Two silhouettes detached from the darkness ahead, guns raised. Our response was swift and brutal. We neutralized the threat without a sound, our presence still cloaked by the shadows.

A door loomed at the end of the corridor, out of

place in its solidity against the dilapidated surroundings. Fucking thing was locked. Whatever was behind it, no one wanted anyone discovering their little treasure. Could Violet be behind the door?

"Stand back." One well-placed kick near the lock, and the door groaned, the barrier splintering under the force of my boots.

The room beyond was a stark contrast to the chaos outside -- pristine, sterile almost, but for one glaring anomaly. The woman in the center of the room. Bound to a chair, her head drooping forward, a gag stifling her cries.

"Vi!" I rushed forward, my hands gentle yet quick as they worked to free her. The tape fell away from her mouth, her breath coming in ragged sobs as she gulped down air.

Then she looked up at me, and I realized I'd been wrong. This woman may have needed to be rescued, but she wasn't my Violet.

"Shh, you're safe now. We got you." I cut through the ropes binding her wrists, my fingers brushing against the marks they'd left. It wasn't her fault she wasn't my woman. She was clearly here against her will, so we'd free her and make sure she was safe. "Can you walk?"

"Y-yeah." She licked her lips. "Thank you for saving me."

"All right, lean on me." She wrapped an arm around my waist, her body trembling against mine as we made our way back out of the warehouse. When we reached the outside, I handed her over to Mock. "Take her to the ER. She needs to be checked out."

Mock nodded. "I'll meet you back at the clubhouse when I'm done."

I got on my bike and went back home. Maybe

Absolem would have something for me. I needed to find her, and it needed to be soon. The longer she was gone, the more likely they'd hurt her. Or worse.

When I got back to the clubhouse, Absolem was huddled over his laptop. His glasses were perched on the bridge of his nose, the glow from the screen casting eerie shadows across his face. He looked up when I came in, his piercing blue eyes scanning my body for any sign of injury.

"Find anything?" My voice was a harsh rasp, fatigue creeping around the edges.

Absolem nodded and gestured me over. "There's another warehouse location, not too far from the one you searched tonight. It's registered under the same company name."

I shook my head. "No. If this one was a bust, then whoever abducted that woman didn't have anything to do with Violet being gone. It's just a coincidence. I already chased one wrong lead. I can't afford to do it again. My gut is telling me this is unrelated."

"Thought you didn't believe in those," he said.

"Usually, I don't. But this time is different. What about what Jo suggested? Any luck tracking Violet's watch?"

Absolem shook his head. "Not yet. I'll try again. Even then, it's not going to be a precise location. But it should get you close."

"That's all I need."

Absolem nodded and got back to work. While everyone tried to help me find Violet, there wasn't much I could do except worry and pace the damn floor. Whenever I found the person responsible for taking Violet, I was going to make them wish they were dead... and then I might actually fulfill that wish.

Wouldn't be the first time I'd killed someone. I'd hoped that part of my life was over, but if I had to get my hands bloody, then so be it. I'd do anything for Violet.

Chapter Twelve
Violet

The coarse rope bit into my wrists, the strands scraping against my skin with each futile twist and pull. Panic clawed at my throat, as I fought against the bindings. Every fiber of my being screamed to break free, to run, to shield the tiny life budding within me from this nightmare.

I had to stay silent, keep my pregnancy hidden behind gritted teeth. My captors weren't aware of the baby, and that ignorance was the only shield I could offer my child. The thought of them discovering my secret, of them possibly using it against me -- it chilled me to the bone.

I clung to silence, knowing that uttering even a single word about the life growing inside me could be more dangerous than the ropes that bound me. I prayed for someone to find us, to make it out of this alive. Not knowing what they wanted was the worst part of it all. What were they planning?

The door creaked open, spilling in a sliver of light that sliced through the darkness. My heart leapt to my throat as three figures emerged from the shadows, their heavy boots thudding on the floor. Their laughter was coarse, grating against my ears as they approached. One of them carried a small lantern.

"Look at her, all scared and trembling," one sneered, his face obscured by a thick beard, his eyes glinting without warmth.

"Like a rabbit caught in a trap." Another chuckled, his leather jacket creaking as he leaned closer, his breath reeking of cigarettes.

"Boss says she'll fetch a pretty price overseas," the third captor said, his voice cold and detached. He had an ugly scar trailing from his eye down to his jaw, a permanent smirk twisted into his rough-hewn features. "Said he'd already had a taste and she was super sweet."

Overseas. The word echoed in my mind, a chilling promise of a fate worse than this dark room. I bit back a sob, not giving them the satisfaction of seeing my fear. They couldn't know about the baby. They couldn't have that power over me.

"Please," I whispered, "don't do this."

"Quiet," the scarred face man snapped, his hand striking out with a swift motion that made me flinch. "You're nothing but cargo."

As they laughed, discussing the details of their vile trade, I shrank back, trying to become invisible. The ropes held me tight, and the thought of escape flickered in my mind. Could I risk it? Could I dare to make a move? First, I'd have to free myself from the ropes.

The baby. My baby. The tiny life inside me depended on every decision I made. Escape meant running, fighting, putting us both in danger. But staying… staying could mean never feeling the freedom of the wind on our faces, the warmth of the sun. My thoughts whirled, each one sharpened with fear.

Not to mention, if I had a daughter, what would they do to her? Would they raise her like cattle to be sold later? The thought sickened me. Bile rose in my throat, and I knew I couldn't let that happen.

Their words caught my attention again. "Boss said this one is special."

What the hell did that mean? What made me different from anyone else they'd done this to?

"She just looks like a hole to fuck," another one

said.

The first one shook his head. "She's apparently got some fight in her. Brother was military. Once Boss had a taste, he put out feelers and found the right buyer. Heard this guy is willing to pay big."

Was that why they'd come for me? Because of how much someone offered to pay for me? It sickened me. Why were there monsters like these in the world?

March will come for us. I had to cling to that hope like a lifeline. Every second felt like an eternity. How long had I been here already?

My eyes darted around the room, searching for anything, any weakness in my captors or the place itself. I had to be smart, wait for the right moment. For my child, I would endure, I would survive. But deep down, I knew I needed to find an opening, and soon. The longer I was here, the more likely I wouldn't make it out of this alive.

I needed to stay strong. For me and my baby. But the strength to fight, to flee, was slipping through my fingers. And then, I heard it. A faint noise outside the door, so soft yet it sent my heart racing with desperate hope. Could it be...? Had March possibly found me?

Had it been hours? Days? I didn't think a week or more had passed. Time didn't mean much here. My sense of time blurred under the dim light that never brightened or faded. Without a single window in this place, I had no way of keeping track of time.

Where are you, March? I pictured his piercing blue eyes, the set line of his jaw when he made a promise. He wasn't just the Underland MC's Sergeant-at-Arms. He was my beacon of hope, and the man I loved with all my heart.

All but one man left the room, leaving the lantern behind. It glowed on the opposite side of the room, the light not quite reaching me, yet still dispelled a lot of the darkness. It made the space a little less frightening.

I remembered the night I first truly connected with March, an unexpected moment of vulnerability from the man who seemed as impervious as steel. He'd let me in and talked about what happened with Ben, and I'd seen the weight he carried. I could only imagine what he was thinking or feeling right now. He must have been terrified, not knowing where I was or if I was even still alive.

March wouldn't fail me. Not when everything was at stake. We'd become so close. It didn't seem fair. Why was this happening? We'd both already suffered so much. Was it wrong for us to try and find happiness? It almost felt like the universe didn't want us to be together.

A rat scurried across the cold floor, its tiny claws scraping. It was a sound I'd grown accustomed to, a companion in my captivity that marked the endless passage of time. I no longer flinched at its presence, my focus solely on the life I was determined to protect.

"March will come," I whispered into the darkness, letting the certainty of those words fill me with a strength I desperately needed. It was all I had left to hold on to.

The chill of the room seeped into my bones, a constant reminder of the cold reality I was trapped in. My breath came out in short puffs, fogging the air before me as I shifted against the bindings that held my wrists tight. Panic fluttered in my chest, but I pushed it down, forced it away with thoughts of warmth and freedom.

The tiny life inside me was oblivious to the danger, and I envied its blissful ignorance. I imagined wrapping my baby in soft blankets, away from this harsh world, where the only noise would be our laughter. I'd foolishly thought this place would be safe once the corrupt officials were gone. But I'd been stupid. Sure, part of me had worried the men who'd raped me might come back, but when all this time passed and nothing happened, I'd thought maybe I was in the clear. There wasn't a single place in this world that could be considered as safe. Evil lurked in the corners and came in all shapes and sizes.

A distant clang echoed through the walls, jolting me from my reverie. My heart skipped a beat. Could it be? *Don't get your hopes up.* But I couldn't help myself. Maybe it *was* March. He wouldn't let me rot here. He promised safety, family. And March always kept his promises.

A shadow moved outside the door, spilled under the crack into the dimly lit space, a fleeting glimpse of something other than the stark walls of my prison. *It has to be him. Please, let it be him.*

I had to believe the club had come to rescue me. If I dared to consider it was just another of the evil men who'd taken me, then I might actually break down and give up hope.

"Come on, March," I muttered, the fight reigniting within me. "Find me." The shadows danced again, taunting me with the possibility of salvation just beyond my reach. Every noise was a potential harbinger of his arrival, every moment stretched thin with waiting.

I closed my eyes, praying this would all be over soon. I wanted to go home, to be with my newfound family. If I was wrong, and March couldn't find me, then I knew my life was about to become a living hell. And I worried the same would be true for my baby.

The sound came again, closer this time -- a rattle

that set my nerves alight. Footsteps? Were those footsteps? My breath hitched, my body tensing as I strained to hear, to identify the source.

And then I heard it, a scraping sound outside the room. My heartbeat thundered, loud enough to drown out all else. This was it. Either my salvation would walk through the door, or my damnation.

The rope against my wrists bit deep, the sting a sharp reminder of each failed attempt to break free. I twisted again, desperation clawing at my resolve. The ropes were relentless, my skin raw from the struggle. Sweat trickled down my temples and spine.

Even when they let me use the bathroom, which wasn't nearly often enough, they kept me trussed up. By some miracle, they hadn't decided to watch. They only gave me small sips of water here and there, and a handful of stale crackers. At this rate, I'd pass out from hunger or dehydration.

I glanced at the man guarding me. He didn't seem concerned about the noise. Did that mean it was more of the men who'd taken me? I squirmed, the chair rocking slightly as I tried to find a way to free myself.

"Quiet down, girl," the man said before spitting on the floor. He watched me, his gaze heavy.

I shimmied against the chair again, searching for any slack, any give in the ropes. Nothing. Panic fluttered in my chest. I couldn't stay here. Not with the baby. Not with what they planned to do. Whether March was coming to save me or not, I couldn't sit and do nothing. I refused to give up.

"Going somewhere?" the man mocked. His footsteps echoed in the semi-dark space as he came closer.

"Please," I choked out, the word dissolving into sobs that I fought to suppress. Tears burned behind my eyelids, demanding release. But I wouldn't break. Not yet. I couldn't. Once I did, then it would all be over. I'd have no hope of escaping.

"Look at her cry." Laughter filled the room, cruel and taunting. "What's the matter? Scared?"

"No," I lied through gritted teeth. But terror filled me with every jeer, each glance that told me I was nothing more than prey. I didn't know for certain whether or not these men would hurt me. They'd left me alone, other than bringing me here and confining me. Would it last much longer?

My head bowed, breaths coming in shallow gasps. I allowed the tears to fall. They streamed unchecked, warm trails that cooled too quickly against my chilled flesh. I cried for my unborn child, for March, for the future I so desperately wanted. And as I poured out all my sorrow and frustration, some of the fear seemed to abate.

The cries subsided, leaving a hollow echo in their wake. Resolve hardened within me, solidifying into a core of steel. I rubbed my face against my shoulders, trying to wipe my tears away. I had to survive. For the baby. For March. He'd nearly broken when we lost Ben. What would happen if I let fear overtake me and I gave up? If he loved me half as much as I loved him, then it would destroy him.

I blinked back the remnants of my tears. Time was a luxury I didn't have. I scanned the dim room, desperate for something, anything that could be a weakness or give me any sort of leverage.

The floor was cold and unyielding beneath my feet. The walls were bare, and from what I could see, there was only the one door into or out of this place. I shifted, testing the give in my restraints. The ropes bit into my wrists, but there had to be a way. Whatever it was, it couldn't draw the attention of the man watching me.

The others returned to the room, whispering to my guard. What did they want now? I tried to keep an eye on them without being obvious about it.

The ropes grazed against my wrists painfully, but I persisted in trying to loosen them, twisting my hands. My skin chafed, a raw sting flaring with each twist. But the pain was nothing compared to the thought of never holding my child or seeing March again.

There. A minuscule slackening in the knot. My pulse quickened with hope. I worked at the rope, millimeter by millimeter. The voices of my captors faded to white noise, my focus narrowing to the fibers gradually yielding to my persistence.

Almost...

Then -- a creak from the hallway. My stomach twisted. I stilled, straining my ears. The thud of boots. My window of opportunity was closing, but the knot was loosening, ever so slightly.

Another creak. Closer now. Adrenaline coursed through my veins, a mix of fear and determination. The rope gave way, just enough for one hand to slip free. A surge of triumph rushed through me, quickly smothered by the impending threat at the door.

The sound of boots stopped right outside. I couldn't afford a mistake -- not now. *Be smart, Vi. Wait for the right moment.*

Silence hung heavy. Then, a faint click, like metal against metal. The doorknob turned slowly, a soft rasp in the quiet. My heart raced, thunderous in my ears. Could it be him? Or just another round of torment?

I watched my guard, but the man seemed oblivious. Or maybe he wasn't concerned. It was possible he didn't believe anyone could take down his buddies. If this was a rescue attempt, then whoever was coming through the door would have the upper hand. Were these bastards so cocky they didn't think they would get caught?

My gaze swung to the door, and my breath hitched as I waited to see who would step through.

Chapter Thirteen
March

I slammed my fist down on the wooden table. Heads turned, eyes locking onto mine. They probably wondered if I'd lost my mind. Truthfully, it felt a bit like I had.

"I need everyone's attention," I barked. One by one they moved closer. Hatter stood beside me, his presence commanding silence without a word. He surveyed the room, every inch the President he was, before meeting my gaze with a curt nod. I stepped back, yielding the floor to him.

"Listen up," Hatter began. "We're about to dive into the lion's den for Violet." His eyes flicked briefly to mine, acknowledging the unspoken worry that gnawed at my gut. "Precision is key. No room for errors."

My jaw clenched as I listened. How the hell had I let her slip through my fingers? I didn't know how they'd lured her out, if they'd infiltrated the clubhouse. Either way, I'd make those fuckers pay. She'd been gone for about three days now. Too long! I worried if we didn't get our hands on her soon, I might never see her again.

"Cheshire and Tweedle," Hatter continued, pointing to where they stood. "Hit the front and make some noise."

"Got it," Cheshire said, flashing his usual grin.

"Rabbit and Mock, keep an eye on the perimeter. Take down anyone who comes out that isn't wearing an Underland MC cut. Or isn't Violet..."

"Understood," Rabbit replied.

"March, you're with me," Hatter said finally, his gaze boring into mine. There was no questioning, no hesitation. Just the calm before the storm. "Knave and Carpenter will stay with the ladies, and I want Absolem at a computer in case we need a…"

"Keyboard cowboy?" Cheshire supplied.

"Yeah, that," Hatter said.

"Copy that," I answered.

"Timing's everything," Hatter pressed on, his eyes scanning the room. "Miss a beat, and it's over for all of us. For Vi. We don't know their exact numbers, or what kind of firepower they have."

"Gear up," I ordered, stepping forward once Hatter finished. The men dispersed, moving with military precision. I watched them go, their steps echoing in the clubhouse.

"March." Hatter's voice cut through the clamor.

"Yeah?" I turned to face him, bracing for what came next.

"Keep your head clear. We need you sharp."

"Always am," I assured him, though the lie tasted bitter on my tongue. With Violet's life in the balance, I couldn't promise to keep my emotions locked down. Not this time.

"Let's bring her home," he said, clapping a hand on my shoulder before striding off to prepare for the fight ahead.

Once everyone had changed and gathered their weapons, we were as ready as we'd ever be. I had my nine millimeter strapped to my thigh, a knife on the other side, and my AR-15 on my back. I was armed to the teeth and would do whatever it took to get my woman back safe and sound.

"We'll bring her back, March," Cheshire said quietly as he passed by, clapping me on the shoulder. I nodded, appreciating his assurance.

"Nothing else matters," was all I said. And it was

the truth.

The hum of the clubhouse faded into a low, menacing growl as I turned away from my brothers. The walls, once a sanctuary, now felt like they were closing in.

"March, time to move," Absolem said, making sure I focused on the here and now.

We rode out, engines growling in the otherwise silent night. She would be safer with us. I would make damn sure of it. Once I got her home, I'd do whatever it took to make sure this sort of thing never happened again. I'd install whatever we needed… cameras, alarms, the works. We should have done this after Jo and Eliza joined us. Then again, no one was after the ladies anymore, and the rest of us hadn't counted on finding someone. I sure the hell hadn't expected Vi to show up, and in trouble at that. We'd all been trained to expect the unexpected. Maybe being civilians was making us soft.

Of course, we should have still put precautions into place. Even though my brothers and I weren't strangers to gun fights, the women were. Every time someone opened fire on us in our damn space, it had to be terrifying for them. Neither Hatter nor Cheshire had brought it up, and the thought hadn't really crossed my mind until now. We clearly needed to do better.

My phone buzzed and I checked it. Absolem had sent the coordinates he'd managed to pull from tracking Violet's watch. I only had to hope they hadn't noticed it on her and removed it. If I got to the location and Violet wasn't there, I was going to seriously lose my shit.

We reached the location, and it looked like an abandoned industrial plant. We'd had to travel about twenty minutes outside of town to get here. Each of us came to a halt and killed the engines on our bikes. The Harley Davidsons were too loud to pull up any closer. I could see two men smoking off to the side, and it looked like another was patrolling the area. That was at least three plus however many were inside.

"Wait for my signal," I commanded. This was it -- the point of no return. But as I looked at the faces of my brothers, their readiness to follow me into hell if needed, I knew we'd bring her home or die trying. Even the Pres nodded, giving me the go ahead. He knew I needed to be in control right now.

I slid the magazine into my Glock with a click. Around me, my brothers did the same. Each of us had donned a Kevlar vest under our cuts. I holstered the Glock and swung my AR off my back. After I double-checked the magazine, I knew it was time.

While Absolem hadn't found as much intel as I'd hoped for, we at least knew where Violet was located. Whoever had her were either ghosts or had hidden their tracks well. Even though we had an idea of what they were up to, and a little bit about their operation, Absolem hadn't found much in the way of details of the men we'd be facing. It made me wonder if they had someone just as gifted with computers who was helping keep them in the shadows.

"Stay sharp," I said. "Watch each other's backs. We didn't survive hell just to die on American soil."

A chorus of affirmations rang out amongst us, bone-deep determination etched on every face. I took one last look at my brothers, the men I considered my family, and nodded. With that, we moved out, each of us blending into the shadows cast by the crumbling buildings like specters on a mission.

We stayed low, our sights trained on the figures lounging lazily against the brick facade of the building.

The scent of stale cigarette smoke hung heavy in the air as we moved closer.

Tweedle and Cheshire were first up. Silent as ghosts, they slipped forward to take out the sentries. The rest of us held position, waiting for their signal that it was clear. I focused on controlled breathing, trying to keep my adrenaline in check.

Suddenly, a choked gurgle broke through the quiet night air, followed by a thud. Before I could even react, another guard was hit out of nowhere. Tweedle and Cheshire had done their job seamlessly, leaving nothing but silence and falling bodies in their wake.

"Clear," Cheshire's voice came through over the earpieces we all wore. I signaled Rabbit and Mock to secure the perimeter while Hatter and I pushed forward toward the entrance of the building.

The door was old and rusted, groaning loudly under our force. My heart pounded against my rib cage as we stepped inside, guns raised and senses heightened.

The interior was as run-down as you'd expect from an abandoned factory -- dusty floors littered with debris and broken machinery creating ominous shadows in the dim industrial lighting. We began clearing room after room methodically, our weapons never wavering from their deadly aim.

"Got something here," Hatter's voice cut through my earpiece as he kicked open a door to reveal a small, makeshift office. Inside, a computer monitor glowed in the darkness.

"Absolem?" Hatter prodded at our tech wizard.

"On it," came Absolem's terse reply over the earpiece. "I'll do what I can to hack into it and see what they've been up to. Keep moving. It looks like Violet is in the building. Check somewhere high up. The signal is too clear for her to be underground."

Without another word, Hatter and I bolted for the stairs, determination and fear fueling our steps. As we approached the top floor, I felt my heart hammering against my chest as though wanting to break free.

I allowed myself to picture her face one last time before swinging my gun up, ready for whatever fight awaited us. There was no way I was leaving this forsaken place without Violet Benson wrapped safely in my arms.

The floor looked to be broken into quadrants. To the right I saw a door slightly ajar, emitting a sliver of sickly yellow light. The smell of stale cigarettes and cheap booze wafted from the gap. Hatter and I shared a look before we moved with a silent understanding, our boots barely making noise against the grimy floor.

Hatter took the lead, his broad form casting an intimidating shadow as he kicked open the door. Gunfire erupted immediately from within the room and I pressed myself against the wall, my heart slamming against my chest. Hatter went down on one knee in response to the attack but quickly rose up, firing back at our unseen assailants.

"March! I'm okay! Go!" Hatter's gruff voice rang through the area as he laid down covering fire. There was no time for hesitation or fear now.

I broke cover and rushed into the room, ready to take down anyone who stood in my way. The room was dirty, furnished sparsely with only a rusty iron bed and a couple of wooden crates that served as tables.

A man stood from a folding chair and I opened fire, taking him out with a head shot and another to the chest. Scanning the area, I checked for any other assailants.

And there she was. My Violet -- tied to a chair in the corner of the room. Her eyes were wide under her dark hair, but she was unharmed, or so it seemed from this distance. Her body shook with fear that I could sense even from where I stood.

I realized, for whatever reason, I couldn't hear much in this room. Not compared to the noise of bullets outside. It made me wonder what this room had been used for originally, because it seemed to have a small amount of soundproofing. It wasn't entirely silent, though. But the noises were definitely muffled.

I dispatched another goon lurking in the periphery before finally allowing my gaze to meet hers. Her eyes sparked with recognition, and relief washed over me like a thick, heady wave. She was safe... for now.

In one swift move, I crossed the room and reached her side, instantly going to work on her bindings. She'd managed to free one hand, but the rope was still secured to her other wrist. The skin looked raw on both, where she'd done her best to free herself. "I've got you, Vi."

Hatter had regained control over his situation and joined us, his sharp gaze assessing Violet for any potential harm. Over the earpiece, we heard Absolem's voice crackling, "Cops incoming... three minutes out. I've accessed what I could off that computer. We can discuss it when you're back."

"We need to move," I snapped, my focus solely on Violet as she tossed the rope aside and stood on shaky legs. I scooped her into my arms, feeling her slight weight against my chest as her arms wound tightly around my neck.

Hatter nodded and cleared a path for us while I

held onto Violet, promising silently to keep her safe. As we made our way out, rounds of gunfire echoed behind us while the Underland MC held their ground. While Hatter and I hadn't had to face off against many, it seemed Cheshire hadn't been so lucky. Although, the grinning bastard seemed to be having fun.

"Ready?" Hatter asked me as we reached our bikes parked a distance away from the factory.

"Just go," I ordered with a glance at Violet who was now seated securely behind me, holding on tight.

As the sirens grew louder in the distance, all of us rode away into the night and back toward safety. I felt Violet press closer to me, her body trembling slightly. Even amidst the lingering fear and uncertainty, there was an undeniable sense of relief that washed over both of us.

We were headed home. Together.

* * *

At the clubhouse, Jo and Eliza came for Violet, leading her away. I knew they'd help her get cleaned up, and they'd let us know if she had any injuries. The look on Absolem's face said we needed to stay and hear what he had to say.

"They were sloppy. From what I was able to access, they'd planned to sell Violet to someone overseas. But it's worse…" He eyed me. "How much do you know about Violet's recent past?"

"Are you asking if I know she was raped?" I asked.

Absolem sighed. "Yeah. Glad it won't come as a shock. The men who hurt her -- and yes, I mean plural -- were apparently testing to see if she'd be a good fit for their plans. It looks like they did the same to nearly a dozen other women. Anyone who fit the requirements of their buyers has either already been rounded up, or they're in the process of it. Looks like they don't go back for them until they think they have a buyer lined up. One of them is in the territory of another club. I sent the info over to them in the hopes they'd be able to extract her in time."

"And the others?" I asked.

"I sent an anonymous tip to the FBI. Even their brightest won't be able to track me. I gave them enough they should be able to save those women, and hopefully round up the assholes responsible. Even if they can't handle the ones overseas, they may be able to convince the agencies who can. Depends on whether those bastards actually give a fuck." Absolem took off his glasses and pinched the bridge of his nose. "Also, I let Sheriff Hurst know about the bodies they'd find at that factory. He's going to cover for us, but I don't know how many times he'll be willing to do something like this."

"Sounds good," Hatter said. "I don't want us mixed up in this any more than we have to be. It's about time we found some peace and quiet."

"I'm going to go check on Vi," I said. Leaving Hatter and Absolem behind, I went to my room, knowing that was likely where Jo and Eliza had taken her. I pushed open the door and found her wrapped in a towel while Jo dabbed ointment on a few cuts.

"She's fine," Eliza said, waving a hand at her. "Just some minor scratches and a few cuts. She may end up bruising. Her wrists were the worst of it thanks to the ropes they used on her."

"I'm good," Violet assured me. "But I wouldn't say no to a sandwich and a nap."

"Then that's exactly what you'll get," I said.

"We're on it." Jo put the medical kit back in my bathroom. "You stay with her. I'll knock when I come back with the food."

"Thanks. Both of you."

They nodded and left, shutting the door behind them. I went to Violet, kneeling at her feet and taking her hands into mine. I studied the wounds on her wrists and kissed the center of her palm.

"You scared the shit out of me."

She gave me a wan smile. "Sorry. I was on my way to the common room when someone grabbed me from behind. I think they came in through the back door."

"We'll make sure that can't happen ever again." I leaned up to kiss her lips softly. "Love you, Vi. I thought I was going to die while you were gone."

"I knew you'd find me," she said, pressing her forehead to mine. "My very own hero."

"Not a hero," I corrected. "Just a man obsessed with his woman."

"Close enough." This time *she* kissed *me*. When Jo came back and knocked on the door, I stood and went to get Vi's food. My hand shook a little as I opened the door.

"If the two of you need anything else, just let us know," Jo said. "No one is going to bother you the rest of the night."

I gave her a nod and shut the door, twisting the lock. I needed to feel like I was blocking out the world. It was only me and Violet right now, and that's how I needed it to be.

Chapter Fourteen
Violet

I awoke with the sharp edge of dawn slicing through the room, but the chill in my bones was soothed by the solid warmth of March's arms around me. His chest was a shield against the creeping light, his heartbeat a steady drum beneath my ear, lulling the remnants of yesterday's terror into silence.

"Morning," he murmured, and I felt the rumble of his voice more than I heard it.

"Morning," I whispered back, not daring to move, as if shifting would shatter the fragile peace that had settled over us.

Someone tried to open the door and March tensed, every muscle coiling like a spring. But then, he heard Absolem's voice call to him. He stood and went to open the door. Absolem glanced at me before focusing on March again. "It's done."

"Done?" I echoed, sitting up. What was he talking about?

"Those bastards won't be breathing anywhere near you again." March folded his arms, looking both protective and intimidating.

"You're safe," Absolem confirmed with a single nod.

I still wasn't sure what that meant. How did he know? No, wait. Did I really want to know? Maybe it was better if I just accepted what he said and left it at that.

"Good." March's response was curt.

Absolem gave one last nod, his blue eyes locking with mine for a moment that seemed to stretch too long, before he disappeared, shutting the door behind him. What had he been trying to convey with that look?

March came back to bed, sliding back under the covers.

"March?"

"Yeah?"

"Thank you." I meant it for everything -- for the safety, for the sanctuary of his arms, for the promise in his eyes. It didn't matter how they knew those men wouldn't bother me again. Whatever they'd done, I'd just accept it.

March wrapped me in his warm embrace. Thanks to him and the men here at the Underland MC, I'd found the courage to hope, to breathe, to stand once more.

March and I went back to bed for another hour or two, but when I knew I wouldn't be falling back to sleep, I got up and showered. After I pulled on some clothes, I left the room to see who else might be awake. I found Jo and Eliza in the kitchen, looking over recipe books.

"What are you two doing?" I asked.

"Thought we'd have a party of sorts tonight. Good food and music. You in?" Jo asked.

"Sure. Just let me know how I can help."

Eliza sighed and shook her head. "Shouldn't have said that. Now she'll have you doing all the kitchen stuff she doesn't like."

"As long as we're all aware I'm a dismal cook, then I'm game for whatever. I can follow instructions. Mostly." We wouldn't discuss the fact that following a recipe often ended in disaster when I was the one cooking or baking.

Jo and Eliza picked out a few desserts for us to make, and Jo got me started on one of them. I sifted flour, the white powder dusting over the wooden countertop like a fresh layer of snow. My hands moved with more surety than they had in days, molding dough as if to reshape my own destiny. I had to admit it was rather fun.

"Looks good," Jo murmured, her voice a low hum beside me. She cracked eggs with a precision that made her seem like a pro.

"Thanks," I replied.

"Can I help?" Eliza's eyes seemed to gleam with happiness. "Jo put me on the sidelines."

"Sure." I patted a spot next to me. "You can help me knead this."

As our hands worked in tandem, kneading and rolling, it felt like we were growing even closer. The scent of baking bread began to fill the air, warm and comforting. I hadn't realized until now how much I needed this.

"Smells like hope," Eliza said, a small smile playing on her lips.

"Hope," I echoed, letting the word sit on my tongue, tasting its sweetness. It was a fragile thing, but it was growing, fed by the nourishment of kindred spirits.

"Damn right," Jo added with a grin. "We'll bake it into every damn loaf, cupcake, and anything else we make. Not only have the three of us had a rough time, but the men here could use some peace as well."

As we baked and cooked, laughter bubbled up, unexpected and bright, as we stood shoulder to shoulder. The hope I'd begun to feel before now blossomed into something more. The future looked far brighter than it ever had. It beckoned like warm sunshine, a path unwinding from the shadows, and I was ready to walk it -- with these women, with the Underland MC, and with March by my side.

Once my part in the kitchen was done, I headed to the common room to help with the decorations. I wasn't entirely sure why we were going all out with this, but it was kind of fun.

I hoisted a string of fairy lights above my head, the tiny bulbs winking like distant stars against the twilight canvas of the clubhouse ceiling. The soft glow cast long shadows on the walls, transforming the place into something otherworldly.

"Higher, Violet," Jo said. I stretched on tiptoes, muscles protesting, attempting to secure the lights.

"What the fuck?" I nearly toppled from the top of the table at Tweedle's outburst. "Why the hell is a pregnant woman doing this? Hell, all of you are pregnant! You should have asked one of us for help."

He came over and helped me down, then hung the lights himself.

"Perfect." Eliza clapped her hands. "It looks amazing in here."

Jo had pushed a few tables together and draped them in red tablecloths. Someone had put on classic rock, but turned the volume down low enough we could all talk and hear each other without shouting.

"Let's get this party started." Cheshire's grin flickered into place as everyone began to file in, their heavy boots thudding against the wooden floor. We still had two tables with chairs we could sit at, and the bar had plenty of room. But we'd opened up the center of the room in case anyone wanted to dance.

Hatter entered and gave me a silent nod. I waved back and wondered what to expect of the evening. I'd thought this would be more a casual buffet type of thing, but it was looking more like an actual party. The longer I was around the club, the more I realized they seemed to celebrate even the small things.

The air soon thrummed with conversation and laughter. The men told tall tales, or talked about funny things that happened while they were in the military. Cheshire pulled Eliza onto the makeshift dance floor, while Jo bustled to and from the kitchen. March stayed beside me, holding my hand.

"Food's ready!" Jo cried out, snagging everyone's attention. March placed his hand at the center of my back and guided me over to the tables of food. He picked up a paper plate and started filling it. When I went to grab one, he tugged me closer.

"This one is yours," he said. "I'll come back for mine."

I stared up at him. "I'm an adult. You know that, right?"

He nodded. "Yep. It did cross my mind, more than once. Especially when I had you digging your nails into my shoulders and screaming my name."

My cheeks flamed and I gasped, glancing around to see who might have heard him. The way Cheshire snickered said he had. Damnit. After March gathered enough food to feed three of me, he set the plate on one of the remaining tables and pulled out a chair for me.

March returned with his own plate as well as a bottle of water for me and a beer for him. He set everything down and claimed the spot next to me. I'd only taken a few bites when Cheshire came over with Eliza, and they sat down in the remaining two seats. I glanced to my right and saw Jo, Hatter, Rabbit, and Absolem were at the other table.

As night deepened, glasses clinked in honor and remembrance as the men lost themselves in the days when they lost brothers. I wondered if this was what family was supposed to be like. Ever since Ben had left to join the Marines, I'd suffered in silence. My home life had been awful, but I'd done my best to endure it. Not once had I ever experienced a true family dinner or holiday. It was starting to look like this would be my first year to get to experience those things.

Cheshire and Eliza got up to dance again, and March scooted closer to me. He tipped his head toward the back hallway, and I nodded. Didn't matter why he wanted to head that way, I was on overload. Too much socializing at once wore me out.

Except he didn't take me out the back door or to our room. Instead, he leaned against the wall and pulled me closer to him. He breathed in my scent and pressed a kiss to the top of my head.

"What's wrong, Marcus?" I asked.

"What happened to you... it tore me up. Even now, I'm scared I'll wake up and this will have been a dream, that you'll still be gone. We were too lax and they were able to come in here and snatch you. Hell, we didn't even realize it. What sort of man does that make me?"

I reached up to cup his cheek. "Clearly, the kind who beats himself up over things we can't change. I don't blame you, not even a little. It happened. They didn't hurt me much. I'll be fine, the baby will be too."

"Let me finish," he interrupted gently, placing his calloused hand over mine. The touch sent a shiver up my spine. "I can't change the past, but I'm here now. And I'm not going anywhere. Ever."

"I --" How could I find the words? How could I tell him that despite everything, he made me feel safe? Cherished? When he said he wasn't ever leaving me, then... did it mean he wanted forever with me? Did I dare hope that's what it meant? The way he'd talked, I'd thought he might, but he hadn't been clear enough. After all, he could have easily grown tired of me at some point and made me leave. This had been his home first.

"All I've ever wanted was to keep you safe. To give you a life far away from the dangers that follow men like me. But damn it, I want you here, with me, always. Keeping my distance was the wrong move. So maybe keeping you by my side is what I need to do." He sighed and pressed his forehead to mine. "I'm not good at this kind of thing, but, Violet Benson, I love you. I know I've said it before, but I want to make sure you know I meant it. I'll tell you a hundred times a day if I need to."

"March..." Love bloomed in my chest, fierce and undeniable. "I love you too."

His smile was full of warmth, the kind that reached deep into my soul and set it ablaze. He leaned in, and his lips met mine in a kiss that spoke of promises and a future I'd never dared to dream of before coming here.

"Whatever comes our way," he murmured against my mouth, "we'll face it together."

"Together," I affirmed, knowing that with him, I could face anything.

He took my hand and led me to the end of the corridor and out the back door. We stepped into the moonlit night, and I breathed in the frosty air. The door shut behind us, but I could still hear the muffled sounds of laughter and music.

"Beautiful night," March murmured, turning to face me.

"Beautiful company," I replied, daring to meet his gaze.

He chuckled, a sound that rumbled through him, and reached up to tuck a loose strand of hair behind my ear. His touch lingered, tracing the line of my jaw before cupping my cheek. I leaned into the warmth of his palm, closing my eyes for a brief moment.

"Can't say I've ever been called that before," he said. "I think you're the one who's beautiful."

I shook my head. I'd never once thought of myself that way, but March had a vitality to him that drew people to him wherever he went. Even here, I saw the way he caught everyone's attention when he entered the room.

His thumb grazed my bottom lip. "I can't promise it'll always be easy --"

"Who wants easy?" I cut him off, opening my eyes to the fierce determination shining in his. "Besides, isn't life supposed to be messy?"

"Damn right." He grinned before his lips descended on mine.

The kiss was everything -- passion and promise entwined. Every fear, every doubt I'd had since coming here, melted away under the intensity of his mouth moving with mine. His arms wrapped around me, pulling me closer until there was no space between us, until I could feel every line of his body pressed to mine.

"March," I gasped when we finally broke apart, both of us breathless. "I love you."

"Love you more, Vi," he vowed. His blue eyes blazed with a fierce protectiveness that seared straight to my soul.

"Show me," I whispered, needing more than words.

And he did. With every kiss, every caress, March reaffirmed the depth of his love. The world outside -- the danger, the uncertainty -- faded away until there was only us, only this moment.

We eventually returned to the celebration, our

hands clasped tightly. The music enveloped us once more, but the dance floor seemed less daunting now. We moved together, lost in the rhythm, surrounded by the family we had found within the Underland MC.

Laughter rang out, glasses clinked, and the savory scent of the feast surrounded us. This was more than a party. It was a celebration of life.

"Home," I said quietly, looking around at the faces illuminated by the flickering lights.

"Home," March agreed, his arm slipping around my waist.

And as the night carried on, with every smile shared and every note played, hope bloomed -- a fierce, unyielding thing. We were part of something indestructible here, bound by loyalty, forged in adversity.

Together, we looked toward a future bright with possibility, cocooned in the love and support of my newfound family. The Underland MC wasn't just a place. It was where my life began anew.

Chapter Fifteen
March

The rumble of my bike's engine died down as I cut the ignition. Vi shifted behind me, and I swung my leg over to dismount, feeling her do the same. We'd been riding for hours, the wind and the road bonding us in ways that words couldn't. I'd woken her early this morning to go for a ride, remembering how much she enjoyed our last one. It wouldn't be long before she'd have to stay off the bike, at least until after the baby arrived. I trusted my driving, but not so much the cars on the road.

"Here we are," I said, glancing at the neon sign flickering above the diner's entrance. "Hungry?"

"Starving," she replied.

We walked side by side, the heavy thud of my boots on the pavement echoing against the quiet buildings. The diner's door jingled sharply as I pushed it open, announcing our presence with far too much cheer. As soon as we stepped inside, the comforting scent of coffee and fried food enveloped us.

"Table for two?" the waitress asked, her smile warm despite the fatigue showing on her face.

"Yeah," I said, my eyes scanning the room out of habit, searching for threats in the corner booths and along the counter. Nothing looked out of place -- just locals and a few truckers mixed in with the smell of grease and the hum of low conversation.

"Follow me," the waitress beckoned, leading us to a booth tucked away in the back. It suited me fine, offering a clear view of the exits and the faces coming in. I slid into the seat, the leather creaking under my weight, and watched as Vi did the same, tucking a strand of dark hair behind her ear.

"Can I get you something to drink while you look over the menu?" the waitress asked, her pen poised over her notepad.

"Water's fine," I answered, knowing Vi would nod in agreement. We didn't come here for the drinks.

"Be right back with those," she said before disappearing toward the kitchen.

Vi leaned forward, resting her elbows on the table, her whiskey-colored eyes searching mine. There was a quiet strength in her gaze, one that hadn't been there before. She'd grown so much since coming here. I was damn proud to call her mine.

The laminated menu felt sticky beneath my fingers. Vi traced the list of pies on the dessert section, a ghost of a smile dancing on her lips. I couldn't help but mirror it. My girl and her sweet tooth! I'd noticed whenever Jo or Eliza baked cookies, Vi was the first to pilfer them.

"Ever had rhubarb pie?" I asked, breaking the silence between us.

"Can't say I have," she replied. "Honestly, it doesn't sound appealing. What the heck is a rhubarb?"

"It's tart, cuts through all the sugar. Like life, I guess." I put the menu down. Analogies weren't my strong suit, but with Vi, words flowed easier than with most.

"Sounds like something worth trying," she said, her eyes locking onto mine with a bravery that belied her cautious nature. "Although, I think I'd prefer the apple."

The waitress returned, pad in hand, ready to take our orders. "What can I get you two lovebirds?"

"Cheeseburger, medium rare, no pickles," I ordered, folding the menu with a snap. My stomach growled in anticipation. Nothing beats diner grub after a long ride.

"Same for me, please," Vi chimed in, her tone growing bolder, more assured with every passing minute.

"Two cheeseburgers, coming up!" The waitress scribbled quickly and collected our menus. "Anything else?"

"Rhubarb pie," we said in unison, and shared a chuckle.

With our order placed, the background chatter of the diner wrapped around us. It was a comforting white noise. Vi fiddled with the salt shaker, spilling grains, then forming little patterns on the worn tabletop.

Our meal arrived, steaming and savory, and we dug in with silent gusto. The burger was perfection -- a juicy patty hugged by a toasted bun. Vi savored each bite like it was her first, and I watched her, fascinated by the joy she found in simple things.

"Good?" I grunted between mouthfuls.

"Amazing," she murmured, her eyes closing briefly in culinary bliss. "Probably not good for me, but it sure hits the spot."

"Heart attack on a plate for sure. Only live once. Might as well enjoy it."

She narrowed her eyes at me. "If you end up with high cholesterol later, I want you to remember this moment. It's fun to eat like this sometimes, but we shouldn't do it all the time."

I smiled, thinking of her nagging me years from now about my diet. It wasn't an unpleasant thought. Well, maybe the no cheeseburger part sucked. I'd never really thought about what my life would look like in the future. Now I had Violet by my side, and a baby on the way. Didn't matter if I was the biological father or not. I planned to be the only dad the little one would know.

We ate, the world narrowing down to the booth, the food, and the company. There was just Vi and me, finding solace in a shared meal and enjoyment in each other's presence. And as we finished the last bites, scraping our plates clean, a sense of camaraderie settled in my chest. This -- right here -- was a slice of normal I hadn't known I craved.

I slid the last bite of pie across my tongue, sweet and tangy. Pushing the plate away, I caught Vi's gaze. She seemed reluctant for our day to end, and so was I. I'd suggested this outing as a way for us to have some alone time that didn't involve a bed. So far, it had paid off. We'd had an amazing day.

"Let's walk it off?" I suggested.

"Sounds perfect," she replied, a soft smile playing on her lips. We left money on the table, enough to cover the meal and a generous tip.

The bell above the diner door jangled as we stepped out into the sunny afternoon. It wouldn't be long before dusk settled over the town, bathing the sky in pinks and oranges. The air was crisp, the kind of freshness you only get after a good meal and the promise of open space.

We made our way toward the park, our steps in sync. My hand found hers, fingers intertwining naturally. Her touch was warm, a stark contrast to the chill that was gradually claiming the day.

"Feels good to stretch my legs," I said, breaking the silence between us.

"Definitely." She squeezed my hand lightly. "And it's nice… this calm. With everything going on, I'd started to think this town would never have something like this. But it's finally over, right?"

I nodded. With the old sheriff gone, and now the mayor and Robert Lewis, things would settle down in Warren. No more girls would go missing off the streets. Sister Mary's shelter wouldn't have as many abused teens and women seeking her help. The town wasn't perfect, and never would be, but at least we'd gotten rid of the worst of the monsters. I couldn't think of a single place that was completely crime free. If someone claimed they knew such a place, I'd still be doubtful. It would be more like no one had discovered what had been happening in the shadows.

Yeah, I was a skeptical bastard. I knew it. Embraced it. Hell, it was part of what kept me alive.

The park was quiet, save for the rustling of leaves underfoot. We walked side by side, shadows growing long as the sun dipped lower. The wind blew through the leaves remaining on the trees, the sound tranquil. I could just picture coming here with our kid once they were old enough to run and play.

"I'm glad we're here right now. Together. It's something I never thought would happen, and now that it has, it's like a dream come true."

"Me too." And I meant it. We didn't need to speak. The clasp of our hands said it all.

We walked until the sun began to set, trailing ribbons of orange and purple across the sky. We trudged along the path that meandered through the park, gravel crunching beneath our boots. The silence wasn't awkward -- it was full, rich with all the unsaid things hanging between us. And we'd have a lifetime to say them.

Ahead, there was a break in the trees. A pond emerged into view, its surface smooth like glass, reflecting the sky. Ducks glided across the water, carefree and unhurried. I marveled at the fact they weren't freezing or hadn't flown farther south for the winter. My heartbeat slowed to match the rhythm of their lazy strokes.

"Look at them," Vi murmured. I followed her gaze, taking in the tranquil scene.

"Peaceful," I agreed. They really were. I could easily sit here and watch them for an hour or more.

We stopped by the water's edge, drawn to the calm it promised. She leaned closer to me, her shoulder brushing mine. Her warmth seeped through the layers of my clothes. Her scent teased my nose, and I realized this was what true happiness was. I gazed down at her and wondered if Ben was watching us right now. Was he happy that we were together? Or was he threatening to kick my ass?

Our eyes met, and something unspoken passed between us. We'd admitted our feelings for one another. Said we wanted a life together. And yet, I hadn't taken the next step. Part of me worried if I would be rushing things. At the same time, I couldn't think of anything I wanted more.

I gave her hand a reassuring squeeze. "Let's stay here a little longer."

"Okay." She leaned her head against my arm, and together we watched the day begin to surrender to night, finding solace in the stillness.

We left the pond behind, the ducks nothing but a fond memory now. Vi's hand was still in mine, as we wandered down the park's winding paths. Nature wrapped around us like a cloak, shielding us from the world beyond. Not that Warren was a bustling city by any means, but here in this park, it felt like we were miles from civilization.

"Beautiful, isn't it?" she asked.

I nodded in agreement, taking in the way

shadows played across her face, softening the hard edges life had etched there. The night was creeping in, but the park glowed with the last vestiges of daylight, casting a golden hue over everything.

"Look at that," Vi said, pointing to a cluster of fireflies beginning to flicker to life. The tiny lights danced between the trees.

"Nature's own spark plugs," I quipped, earning a chuckle from her. It felt good, natural, to make her laugh. To find a moment's rest from the weight of my responsibilities.

"March, what's that over there?" Her eyes caught something I hadn't noticed -- a pet store, nestled between the greenery and the encroaching urban landscape.

"Let's check it out." The words were out before I could second-guess them. I steered us toward the shop, curiosity piqued. Even though we'd been in Warren for quite a while now, I'd never noticed this place before. Of course, until Luna showed up in my life, I hadn't had a reason to.

"Could be fun," she said with a playful nudge against my side, her eyes lighting up with the prospect of something ordinary, something normal.

"Never know what you'll find," I replied, feeling an unexpected thrill at the idea of stumbling upon hidden treasures within those four walls. There's strength in the small things, the unplanned detours. They remind you there's more to life.

The neon sign of the pet store flickered as we approached, its buzz barely audible. We stood outside for a heartbeat, looking through the window.

"Ready to be surprised?" I asked, but it wasn't about what lay inside. It was about the possibility that unfolded whenever we were together -- unexpected, uncharted, unreal.

"Always," Vi answered, squeezing my hand once more before we stepped through the door, ready for our next adventure.

The bell above the door jangled sharply as we entered. A chorus of barks and chirps greeted us, a wild chorus that set the cramped space alive. I scanned the familiar chaos of a pet store -- cages and tanks stacked upon shelves, the smell of sawdust and kibble thick in the air.

"Look at them," Vi whispered, awe coloring her usually cautious voice.

I followed her gaze to a large tank where a bearded dragon sprawled lazily atop a rock, its eyes half-closed, indifferent to our presence. She chuckled softly, the sound cutting through the animal cacophony. Her laughter always hit me hard, like a fist to the chest -- a welcome punch.

"Let's see the kittens," I suggested. The tension that laced my spine began to ease with each step deeper into the store.

We turned a corner and there they were -- the kittens. Huddled together in a cardboard box, tiny bodies jostling for warmth. Their mews were desperate, high-pitched calls for attention. Calls for someone to care. Vi's face softened as she watched them, and I sensed her urge to protect, to comfort. It mirrored my own instincts.

"March, they're so small," she murmured, reaching out a tentative hand. Her touch was gentle, and one braver kitten sniffed her fingers before letting out a hopeful squeak. I saw the pull in her eyes, the need to give these creatures a piece of the safety she'd recently found.

"Abandoned," I said flatly, the word leaving a

sour taste. Too close to home. Unwanted, left behind. The sign on the box said as much.

Vi nodded. "They didn't choose this. I wonder if they were taken from their mom?"

"It's possible," I replied, my voice low, almost lost among the plaintive cries. Amid the mewling clatter, one little life stood out. A blaze of orange among shades of gray, black, and white.

Vi's breath hitched audibly, her hand stilled in mid-air. "Look…"

"Fiery little guy," I murmured, watching as the tabby batted at her outstretched finger with a paw, more playful than its siblings. Its fur was a bright splash of color, like sunshine fighting through storm clouds.

"March," she whispered, her voice quivering with something I couldn't place -- a mix of hope and heartache. "This one."

"Sure?" My query was rough-edged, tinged with the gravity of what she was asking. To take this creature under our wing, to shelter it from the storm -- it wasn't a decision to make lightly. We already had Luna at home, and a baby on the way. I wasn't sure we needed the extra responsibility, but I also knew I could never tell her no.

Vi nodded, her eyes never leaving the kitten. There was no hesitation. Only certainty. A commitment forming without words spoken aloud. She understood the stakes, the responsibility. So did I.

"Let's do it." Her smile cracked through her usual caution, a rare beam of unguarded joy. "We'll call him Shine."

"Shine," I echoed, a chuckle escaping me despite the tightness in my chest. It felt like a promise, a vow made not just to the tabby but to ourselves. To foster light in the darkness we knew all too well.

"Looks like you're part of the family now, little one." I reached into the box. The kitten's bright eyes met mine, a silent acceptance in his gaze.

"Welcome to the family, Shine."

In addition to the kitten, we grabbed some toys and two collars. After I paid, we headed outside. The jingle of the store's bell faded behind us as I cradled Shine in my arms, his small body vibrating with purrs.

"Needs a bed too. Something soft. And a scratching post." I knew we couldn't fit it all on my bike, so we'd have to get some things delivered. For now, we had enough. The thought of Luna's reaction sparked a rare grin on my face. I'd felt bad that we never seemed to be able to play with her enough. Now she'd have a sibling to torment.

Outside, the cool air embraced us. We walked side by side, the weight of the kitten a welcome one. I'd close him up inside my cut on the way home and drive slow. It would have been better if we'd been in Violet's car, but I hadn't exactly planned to adopt another cat.

"Think Luna will be okay with a little brother?" Vi's question broke the silence.

"Guess we'll find out soon enough," I replied, the corner of my mouth twitching upward. I could picture it -- the wariness, the curiosity, and then acceptance. A bond forming, just as ours had. Or they could be like some siblings and fight constantly. We wouldn't know until we introduced them. I definitely needed to get a vet appointment set for them both to get their shots and schedule their sterilization surgery. The last thing we needed was more kittens.

"Let's head back," I said, the engine roaring to life beneath me, the sound a familiar comfort. I zipped the kitten up and placed Violet's hands over it once she'd wrapped them around my waist. Then I eased forward and headed back to the clubhouse.

The road unfurled before us as we rode back to the Underland MC to introduce Shine to Luna.

"Welcome to the ride of your life, Shine," I murmured. I wondered if it would be possible to teach him to ride with us like this. Might be fun. Luna, on the other hand, would be too terrified. I could tell from her personality. But this one... he seemed different.

Vi snuggled into me, and my bike ate up the miles until we passed through the gates to the Underland MC. I had a feeling my brothers were about to give me shit for bringing another cat home.

Chapter Sixteen

Violet

Shine pounced, and the catnip mouse skittered across the floor. I couldn't help but smile, as I watched March's fingers deftly teasing the little tabby with the toy. Luna, our other kitten, regarded her sibling with cool disinterest from my lap.

"Come on, Shine," March coaxed, his voice a soft rumble, so different from the authority it carried during club meetings. The kitten leaped, all clumsy enthusiasm, and batted the mouse back to him.

I stroked Luna's sleek fur, feeling her purr vibrating against my palm. My mind drifted, worry gnawing at me despite the momentary peace. I glanced around the room. It was cozy, intimate, but space was a luxury we didn't have.

"Where do you see us in a few years?" I asked.

He caught the mouse as Shine returned it, pausing to look at me. "We'll figure it out. You know that."

"Raising our baby here, around the club feels right," I confessed, my gaze flickering to my still mostly flat belly, then back to his steady face. "But there's not enough room here. Not for everyone."

"Underland is more than walls and rooms," he said, standing up and stretching his broad shoulders. "It's family. And for family, we make space."

I nodded, wanting to believe. "Okay."

I trusted him, more than anyone. But the fear of the unknown, of cramped quarters and kids without their own corners to grow -- it weighed on me. They might not have a normal life by the average person's standards, but I still wanted to give our baby the best life I could. And I wasn't sure we were able to do that right now.

"Trust me," March said. "I'll talk to Hatter. We'll find a way to make this work. I'm sure Jo and Eliza have wondered the same thing."

"Okay," I repeated, holding onto his words and the certainty they brought. Luna nuzzled into my hand, demanding more attention, pulling me back to the present. For now, we had enough room for love and growing kittens. That had to be enough.

March's hand found mine, his grip firm and reassuring. "I'm going to talk to Hatter," he said, his voice low and resolute. "And I mean that as in right now. We'll work something out for us -- for the baby. You asked where I saw us, but where do you see us, Vi? What are your dreams?"

I leaned into him, the rough texture of his cut a contrast against my skin. "Just this. Being with you is all I've ever wanted. More than any dream."

"Even if we never leave this place?" His eyes searched mine, looking for the truth beneath the words. I could understand his concern. I'd never left home until now. He probably worried I'd want to travel or move somewhere more exciting than a sleepy little mountain town.

"Even then." I paused. "Before, when I was a little girl, I used to wonder what my wedding would look like. White dress, flowers. The usual I guess. Only one thing never changed. You. It was always you I dreamed of marrying."

His laugh was a soft rumble in his chest. "Nothing about us is traditional, Vi. Doesn't mean you have to give up on those dreams, though."

"True." I smiled. "But I don't need a wedding, March. As long as I have you, as long as we're together, that's what matters."

His lips curved in a smile that didn't quite reach his eyes. I could tell my answer bothered him for some reason. Did he feel like I was giving up something important to be here with him? Because I wasn't. Without him, I didn't have a future worth mentioning.

* * *

March

As Violet's laughter melded with the playful squeaks and mews of the kittens, I stood and slipped away, leaving her ensconced in a world of innocent joy.

The kitchen was thick with the scent of coffee and the low hum of serious conversation as I stepped into the room. Hatter leaned back against the counter, his posture relaxed but eyes sharp. Cheshire sat at the table, a half-smirk playing on his lips, while Rabbit fidgeted with a pen cap. Absolem's glasses caught the light, a glint of focus in his gaze.

"Space," I said, cutting through the murmur. "We're running out of it."

Hatter nodded slowly. "Our family is growing and we need some changes. We've discussed it before, but it's time to get more serious about it."

"Vi and I..." My voice trailed off. "We need a plan."

"Expansion." Absolem's voice was calm and quiet. "Clear some trees, make room for tiny homes."

"Tiny homes?" Rabbit's eyebrow shot up, his voice jittery.

"Close to the clubhouse," Absolem continued. "Keep everyone together but give them space."

"Community," Cheshire mused, his grin widening. "Still together, but with room to breathe."

"Let's walk the land tomorrow," Hatter decided.

"See what we're working with."

Cheshire tilted his head. "Tiny homes are fine for now, but what about when families expand? We can't have our brothers crammed like sardines. A tiny home may work if you just have one kid. What if you have three or four?"

I nodded in agreement, feeling the tension knot in my stomach. I personally wouldn't mind one of those homes, but Violet and I hadn't really talked about how many kids we wanted. Cheshire had a good point. A tiny house might not work if we had a bunch of kids. Hell, I wasn't sure I wouldn't screw up *one* kid, much less a herd of them.

"Two, maybe three bedrooms, then," I suggested, trying to picture kids running around, laughter weaving through the walls of a home. "Keep them snug but not suffocating."

"Between one thousand and twelve hundred square feet," Cheshire added, leaning forward, his elbows on the scarred wood of the table. "Enough room to grow without losing our closeness, and without spending a fortune on the construction."

"Modular homes," Absolem interrupted, his voice steady as always. The glasses perched on his nose gave him that look -- like he'd already solved the problem before we even knew there was one. "Fast to set up. Efficient."

"Modular…" Hatter mused, his brow furrowing slightly. "We do need quick solutions. Families can't wait."

"Exactly," Absolem agreed, tapping a finger against the table. "I'll get the specs, find a vendor. We buy in bulk so we can negotiate."

"Good call. I'll mark off the lots with you. Once we have a plan, we get the trees cleared and meet with the sellers."

"Strike a deal," I said, the idea taking hold. "Give everyone a piece of something real."

"Something theirs," Cheshire echoed, his smile less mischievous now, more genuine. "I'm good with that. Bet Eliza will be too."

We knew we were building more than houses. We were crafting a future. None of us had ever thought about settling down. When we moved here, we'd assumed we'd all be bachelors the rest of our lives. But things were rapidly changing, and for the better.

"I've got some cash saved up," I said, thinking about the money in my account. But Absolem was already shaking his head, a sly grin tugging at his lips.

"Better idea." He adjusted his glasses, eyes sharp behind the lenses. "The ex-sheriff, the mayor -- they've got accounts swollen with dirty money. Remember how I snagged some hidden funds before?"

"Absolem, you thinking what I think you are?" Hatter leaned in, interest piqued.

"Exactly that. A little financial retribution." Absolem nodded. "The FBI will be watching anything to do with the mayor. That one might be tricky, but finding other assholes like him should be easy enough. No reason we can't swipe their money. Doesn't have to be someone we helped take down. I can search for predators and wipe their accounts before they even realize what's happened. It will make it harder for them to operate as well."

"Robbing hoodlums to house our own," Cheshire quipped, a spark of admiration in his tone.

"Damn right," I agreed, heart hammering with the prospect. It was justice, served cold and hard. And no, I had no qualms about using dirty money, not if we put it to good use. If there was enough, we could also use it to help out around town. Donate some to Sister Mary. Buy groceries for a family in need, or for the food pantry. Lots of possibilities. "Let's do it."

"It's unanimous, then," Hatter said.

"Stealing from scumbags isn't theft, it's a public service." Cheshire snorted at my comment. I stood now that a decision had been made. I left my brothers and returned to Violet.

Back at the room, the sight made me pause. There she was, my Violet, curled up safe and snug on the bed, her chest rising and falling in a quiet rhythm. Luna and Shine, those little bundles of fur, nestled close to her warmth, all three lost to dreams.

Silently, I slipped off my boots and joined them. Soon, we'd have more than just this room -- more than just dreams. We'd have a real future, one I'd fight for with every breath, every dollar, every stolen cent.

I leaned in, my lips brushing Vi's cheek softly. "I love you," I murmured into the delicate shell of her ear, my breath stirring a few strands of her dark hair. She stirred ever so slightly, a soft sigh escaping her lips. Contentment washed over me as I stretched out beside her, my body a careful distance away to not wake her. I watched the steady rise and fall of her chest, lulling my own heart into a quiet calm.

The nightmares that once haunted her sleep had become a rare occurrence. She was at peace now. The kittens, Luna and Shine, formed a tiny, purring barrier between us. Their innocence was a stark contrast to the grit and grime outside these walls. It was a contrast I would protect with everything I had.

My gaze lingered on Vi's face, the soft curve of her jawline, the fall of her eyelashes against her pale cheeks. Could I give her more? The question loomed in my mind, heavy and insistent. A ring... No, a vow.

Marriage. It would mean giving the baby my name, wrapping them both in an unbreakable bond to me. And for Vi, it would be a testament -- a promise that my commitment was as enduring as the stone in an engagement ring.

Quietly, I pulled my phone from my pocket, my fingers deft as they navigated through searches. Engagement rings. My eyes flitted over countless images, each sparkling band and gleaming gem whispering promises of forever. This wasn't about tradition or appearances. This was about staking a claim, declaring to the world that Violet Benson was mine, and I was hers, now and always.

A simple band caught my eye, with a few diamond chips embedded in it. Elegant. Strong. Like her. I bookmarked the page, my heart thumping at the possibility of legally making her mine. For her, for our future, I'd ride into hell and back. Asking her to marry me seemed like a small thing in comparison. But I suddenly wanted that more than anything. Would she? She'd said she didn't need a wedding, but I wondered if she really wanted one and was just too afraid to ask for it.

All I needed was for her to say yes. The thought soothed me in a way I couldn't really understand. Being with Violet had changed me more than I had ever imagined. It wasn't just about surviving anymore but about living -- breathing easy knowing whatever may come our way, we would face it together.

The decision was made then. There wasn't much left to think about now. Once she woke up, I'd ask. Or maybe I needed to make the moment special. Find the right time. I didn't want to half-ass this. Now that I'd made up my mind, I wanted to make sure I did it right.

I checked the ring on my phone again. I'd buy it right now, except I had no idea what size she wore. And I couldn't think of a way to figure it out without giving away my intentions.

My gaze lingered on her hand resting on her belly. The sight made my chest tighten, love for her and our unborn child swelling in me. And yes, it was *my* child and I dared anyone to say otherwise.

A rough sigh escaped me as I skimmed through more rings, my mind wandering to places and moments where I could propose. A dinner date at some fancy restaurant? No. Violet seemed more at home here, within the familiar walls of the club, surrounded by people who cared for her. A picnic under the stars, perhaps? Or maybe right here in this room, a quiet moment between just the two of us... Why the hell was this so difficult?

"Fuck," I muttered under my breath. This was going to be tricky.

The kittens purred louder from where they nestled against Vi's body. They had it easy -- no complications or struggles about rings and sizes.

My gaze trailed down to their small furry bodies, a thought sparking in my mind. Luna's collar... it was made out of a thin leather strap with a small buckle that could be adjusted as she grew.

A wily grin spread across my face as I stared at the tiny leather collar buckled around Luna's neck. It wasn't perfect, but it could work as a makeshift measure.

I slid from the bed as quietly as I could manage, careful not to disturb Violet or her furry companions. Crouching down beside Luna, I gently lifted the small kitten into my hands, feeling her tiny heart fluttering against my palm.

"All right, Luna," I whispered, "let's see what we can do."

With a nimble, careful touch, I unbuckled the leather collar and looped it around Violet's ring finger. It slipped on easily enough, and with some minor adjustments, I managed to fit it around her finger.

Content with the rough size estimate, I slipped off the collar and carefully traced the circle on a piece of paper before I re-fastened the leather around Luna's neck. She gave a muted purr as I set her back down beside Vi, her tail flicking lightly against my hand.

Pulling out my phone again, I found a printable sheet that would help me determine her ring size. I got up and went to Hatter's office so I could print the sheet. Once I had it in hand, I used it to measure the circle I'd drawn and determined what size Violet wore.

With that done, I made my final decision on a ring and made my purchase. Best part was that the store was local and they offered delivery. I'd have the ring in my hands within the next hour or two.

Now I just needed to decide when and how to propose to her. Maybe on a moonlit bike ride? Or a big production in front of our family? No. I didn't think Vi would really enjoy being in the spotlight like that. The ride might be better. Just the two of us, and the sooner the better.

Chapter Seventeen
March

The stars and moon shone above us in the night sky as I gripped Vi's hands. Her eyes, glassy with unshed tears, focused on mine. My brothers, along with Jo and Eliza, stood silently. My heart hammered like a piston in my chest, nerves twisted with a love so fierce it almost hurt.

"March, do you take Violet to be your lawfully wedded wife?" Hatter's voice was steady, but emotion tinged its edges. The Pres had been licensed online in order to preside over my wedding to Violet. I really owed him one this time.

"Without a doubt. I take her, all of her -- past, present, and future."

Vi's fingers trembled in mine, but her spirit, that resilient flame inside her, burned bright enough for both of us.

"And you, Vi? Do you take March to be your lawfully wedded husband?"

She nodded, words catching in her throat before spilling out soft and clear. "I do. In every way, I do."

We slipped the rings onto each other's fingers -- a symbol of our love and devotion. My thumb brushed over her knuckles, wanting to savor this moment.

"Forever, March," she whispered, her voice a beacon through any storm. "I want to be with you until the very end."

"Forever," I promised back, sealing our vows with a kiss that had my brothers whistling and stomping their boots.

The roar of applause and the rev of engines filled the air as Vi and I turned to face our Underland MC family. Hatter's voice boomed over the crowd, "I now pronounce you man and wife!"

"Brother, you did good!" Cheshire clapped my back, his mischievous grin wider than ever. Absolem, silent as always, nodded with approval, the rare smile on his face worth a thousand words. They stood close, witnesses to our union. Having them here meant the world to me, and they knew it.

"Welcome to the family, Vi," Cheshire said, his tone laced with warmth beneath the usual sarcasm. She smiled up at him, a genuine connection sparking as she found her place among us.

"Thank you. All of you." Her voice trembled with emotion, but it was strong, too -- like her.

"Let's celebrate!" someone shouted, and everyone headed inside, where Jo and Eliza had prepared some food.

"Ready for the next adventure?" I whispered to Vi as the noise rose around us.

"Always," she answered, eyes gleaming with curiosity and trust.

"Close your eyes then." I reached for the bandana in my pocket, feeling her surprise as I tied it gently over her eyes. Her hands found mine, gripping tightly.

"March? What are you --"

"Shh, just trust me." My heart raced again, this time with anticipation for what lay ahead.

"Is that... a motorcycle?" Her excitement was palpable even through the blindfold. Her fingers trailed over the leather seat.

"Got it in one," I chuckled, helping her onto the bike before swinging a leg over myself. The engine rumbled to life beneath us.

"Where are we going?" Her voice danced with excitement, the thrill of the unknown making her words quiver.

"Somewhere where it's just you and me." I felt her nod against my back, her arms wrapping around my waist. "And don't worry. Eliza and Jo said they'd take care of Shine and Luna for us."

"Let's go, then," she pressed, and I didn't need another word.

Pulling out of the lot, I glanced back at our family, their cheers still ringing in my ears.

Asphalt blurred beneath us, a winding serpent that carved through the heart of the mountains. I twisted the throttle, and the bike roared its approval, devouring each curve with a ravenous hunger. Vi clung to me, her body pressed tight against my back as we leaned into another hairpin turn. The wind tore at us, wild and relentless, but it was freedom that screamed in our ears, that flooded our veins.

"It's incredible!" Vi yelled, still blindfolded but enjoying the ride just the same.

"Wait until you see the view," I shouted back over my shoulder, my words snatched away by the rush of air. Trees flashed past in a blur of green under the moonlight.

The bike thrummed beneath us, a beast of chrome and leather, and I felt every pulse of its power resonate with my own heartbeat. We flew past rocky outcrops, the scent of pine sharp in my nostrils. My focus was absolute -- on the road, on the woman I loved, on the life we were racing toward.

Finally, we broke free from the embrace of the forest, and ahead lay our sanctuary. Nestled among trees that had stood watch for centuries was the cabin -- a promise of solitude made of wood and stone. I killed the engine, and silence descended like the first snowfall of winter.

"Are we here?" Vi's voice was hushed, reverent even without sight.

"Open your eyes," I said, unwinding the bandana from around her head with careful fingers.

She blinked, eyes wide as she took in the cabin. It stood humble yet proud, a chimney stack that promised warmth, windows glowing like amber. The porch creaked as we walked up to the door. It felt as if the cabin itself had been waiting for our arrival.

"It's..." She trailed off, lost for words.

"Ours," I finished for her, taking her hand and leading her inside.

The interior was all rich woods and soft fabrics, a fire already crackling merrily in the hearth. A bed, large and beckoning, was piled high with quilts, while the back windows offered glimpses of a world untouched, untamed.

"Welcome home, Vi." My voice was a growl of contentment, resonating within the wooden walls.

"Home?" she echoed. Her gaze scanned the cabin, taking it all in.

"I bought this place. It's more of a weekend getaway type of cabin. There's a full bathroom, an efficiency-size kitchen, and one hell of a view. Thought it would be the perfect spot for a honeymoon."

My fingers brushed hers, calloused but gentle, and I watched her shoulders relax beneath my touch. Each breath she took seemed to draw in the quiet and stillness of the mountain.

She turned into my embrace. Her warmth seeped into my bones, a balm to the chill in the air. Our foreheads touched. The world outside faded until there was only this: the shared heartbeat, the unspoken promises, the tapestry of scars we carried. We were the sum of our battles, our love hard-won and fierce.

Her gaze held mine. She didn't have to say a word. I could practically read her thoughts. We'd had our wedding today, and someone important had been missing, but we knew Ben would want us to be happy.

I loved her so damn much. She saw through the soldier and the biker to the man beneath.

Our lips met, a tender clash of souls hungry for contact. I tasted her, the sweet tang of new beginnings, and felt something shift inside me -- a release of every tightly wound coil. In her kiss, I found absolution.

This cabin would be our sanctuary, and for tonight, it would give us the privacy we craved on our special day. We shed our clothes, discarding them on the wooden floor. I planned to worship her body all night and into the morning, adoring every single part of her.

I couldn't help but admire the perfection of my wife. She had the prettiest fucking body I've ever seen. Her breasts were perfect handfuls, and I couldn't wait to suck on them. The way her hips swayed as she walked always made me want to rip off her clothes and bury myself inside her right then and there.

Without a word, I pinned her against the wall, my hard cock pressing into her soft stomach. I wanted her to know who was in charge here.

"You're mine tonight," I whispered into her ear, my free hand tracing delicate circles around her nipple. She shivered in response, arching her back against me.

"Yes," she moaned, "please."

I pulled away from her slightly, giving myself enough room to admire the view. My cock twitched at the sight of her curves. Fuck! I couldn't wait any longer.

I grabbed both sides of her head and crashed my lips down onto hers again, forcing my tongue into her mouth. She met my kiss with equal fervor, moaning as she ran her hands over my chest and down my abs.

I pushed her back onto the bed and climbed on top of her, pinning both of her wrists above her head with one hand while using the other to tease one of those perfect nipples with my thumb and forefinger. She squirmed beneath me, arching into my touch as if begging for more.

"You like that?" I asked, leaning down to lick along the line of her jawbone up toward her earlobe before nipping at it gently with my teeth. She whimpered softly in response, nodding frantically.

I continued to torment those perfect tits with my hands while moving lower until I was hovering over her quivering stomach. My cock was aching for release, but I wasn't going to give in just yet. This was going to be a long night filled with pleasure for both of us.

I eased a hand down between her legs, parting her slick pussy. Her hard little clit practically begged for attention. Using my shoulders to spread her thighs wider, I leaned in and lapped at her sweet honey.

"Marcus!" Her hips thrust up, and I sank a finger into her, pumping it in and out slowly. As I tormented my sweet new wife, I made her come not once, not twice, but three times.

I settled over her and eased my cock into her. Her legs went around my waist, pulling me in deeper. Her soft cries filled the cabin as I thrust into her. It wasn't our first time together, and yet it felt different. Knowing she was my wife changed things.

I didn't think I'd be able to hold back and took her harder and faster. The moment her pussy squeezed my cock, I knew I was done for. Gripping her hips tight, I powered into her, not stopping until every last drop of cum had been wrung from my balls.

Afterward, we lay panting on the bed, and I pulled her into my arms. It may have ended quickly, but I wasn't done. Not by a long shot. We'd rest a bit, I'd feed her, and then we'd go for round two.

"Thank you," she whispered, her voice a soft caress in the quiet room. "For everything."

I stroked her hair, dark strands slipping through my fingers. "No need for thanks. It's us now. You and me. We're a package deal."

She lifted her gaze to mine. "You've given me a home, a family."

* * *

The days melded into one another, each moment a treasure. We cooked together, laughter echoing as flour dusted our clothes and faces. She danced around the kitchen, a graceful whirlwind, while I watched, captivated.

"Try this," she said, offering a spoonful of sauce. Its rich flavor burst on my tongue, as surprising and delightful as the woman before me. It looked like she'd been picking up a few things from Jo and Eliza.

"Perfect," I declared, not just speaking of the food.

After we ate, we wandered through the forest. Birds serenaded us, their songs weaving through the canopy above. Sunlight dappled Vi's skin, turning it golden, and I couldn't resist pulling her close for a kiss.

"Beautiful," I murmured, eyes locked on hers, not the scenery.

"March," she laughed, cheeks flushing with pleasure, "you're biased."

"Guilty."

She leaned into my touch. "I can't believe we're here. That I'm here... with you."

"Believe it. You're my strength, my calm in the

storm." I tightened my hold on her. "You make the Underland MC not just a club, but a home."

"Your home is my home."

"We'll keep riding together. Build something solid for the future, for our little one."

"Within the club," she said, "we'll raise our child to know loyalty, respect... and love."

"Love above all," I confirmed. Our dreams, once ghosts in the wind, now had substance. They were tangible things we could chase down.

* * *

After we'd been at the cabin nearly a week, I knew it was time to head back. Dawn broke as we packed up our few belongings.

"Ready to head back?" Vi asked.

"Let's do it." I stowed our things in my saddlebags, then swung my leg over the bike, the engine rumbling to life beneath us as I started it. She climbed behind me, arms circling my waist.

We descended the mountain. Each curve, each dip, brought us closer to what awaited. We were in this together now, until the very end. Because now that I'd made her mine, I wasn't ever letting her go.

The gates of the Underland MC came into view. We rolled in, the roar of the bike declaring our return.

As we dismounted, the reality of our world settled on us -- a world of danger and uncertainty, but also of boundless love and fierce loyalty. We'd face it together along with the rest of the Underland MC. Hand in hand, we stepped forward, ready for whatever lay ahead.

Chapter Eighteen
Violet

Coming back not just as Violet, but as March's wife, had my stomach fluttering with nerves. The clubhouse seemed quieter than usual. My hand trembled as I pushed open the door and stepped inside. The familiar scents of coffee, leather, and oil greeted my nose, wrapping around me like a comforting embrace.

"Vi!" Jo's voice rang out and I found her hurrying toward me from the kitchen.

Her smile was infectious as she approached. My heart swelled seeing her again. We'd only been gone about a week, but it felt too long now that we were back. Eliza was right beside her, her own grin just as wide, and something soft flickered in her eyes. I hadn't been part of the Underland MC for very long, and yet they both looked so happy to see me. It made me realize these women weren't just friends. They were my sisters.

"Come on," Eliza urged. "We have something to show you!"

March gave me a nod and I scurried after the two of them. They led me to the spare room I'd been using, its door closed. Jo's hand rested on the knob. She threw a quick glance at Eliza, an unspoken conversation passing between them.

"Ready?" Eliza asked, her words soft but laced with an energy that made my pulse quicken.

"More than ever," I replied, anxious to see what they were hiding behind the door.

With a nod, Jo turned the handle, and the door swung open.

My breath caught -- three cribs sat along one

wall. A colorful rug covered the center of the room, and I saw a changing table, three rocking chairs, and a handful of baby toys still in the packages. I stepped inside, my heart pounding a fierce rhythm against my ribs.

"Jo… Eliza…" The words stumbled out, tripping over the swell of emotions that surged like a tide within me.

"Vi, do you like it?" Jo asked. "The club worked on it while you were gone."

"Like it?" I echoed, laughter bubbling up from a well of happiness. "I'm… overwhelmed."

I turned, taking them in -- two pillars of resilience who'd become my sisters in ways blood never defined. Their smiles were my lifeline, their presence my sanctuary. We closed the distance in a few heartbeats and hugged each other so tight.

"Thank you," I murmured into the softness of Jo's hair, her scent mingling with Eliza's. "For everything."

"Family looks after family." Eliza's words were simple, her conviction unyielding. "The guys wanted us to feel like us and our children will always have a place here, even if we aren't all living together in the clubhouse. This room will always be a place the kids can come and play together."

We stood there, tangled in an embrace that spoke more than any words ever could. This was home. This was where futures were forged -- not in the chaos outside, but in the quiet moments that stitched our souls together. Here, in this nursery, hope bloomed anew, nurtured by the hands of those who knew the price of survival all too well.

I heard the thump of boots heading our way and turned to see Hatter, Cheshire, and Absolem. I wasn't sure where March was, but my guess was that he was catching up with everyone else.

"Have you told her yet?" Hatter asked.

Jo and Eliza shook their heads. What else had they been planning while we were gone?

Cheshire's grin flashed. "Big plans for our little slice of heaven here. We started to discuss it before you left but finalized a few things this past week."

"Modular homes." Absolem's words were succinct, the excitement in his eyes barely contained behind those steel-rimmed glasses.

I blinked, trying to process the quick shift in topics. "Modular homes?"

"Community living," Hatter clarified, crossing his arms over his chest. The scars on his face seemed to deepen with his serious expression. "A way to keep us all close and safe, yet give us some privacy and space to grow."

"Reckless Kings offered up their plans," Absolem continued, leaning back against the doorframe. "But we're Underland. We're not like them. It's possible things may change down the road and we'll want something different, but for now, this is the quickest and best option for the club."

Cheshire's eyes sparkled. "Nothing big or fancy. Three-bedroom homes that are twelve hundred square feet or smaller. Even the single guys will get them, in case they find women and decide to start families. We're going to clear out some trees, run whatever pipes or wires we need to prep the space, and Hatter has been working on a deal with a modular home place just down the highway."

Their visions of the future, strong and unwavering, filled the room with an electric charge. They wanted to build a community not of isolation, but of collective strength. I liked it. Even if we weren't all sharing the same space anymore, it would be like a close-knit neighborhood all on Underland MC property.

"Close to the clubhouse," Hatter said, "but with enough space to call it your own. We'll put in a playground nearby once the kids are a little bigger. If anyone wants to get a dog, we can put up fencing for small backyards."

Hatter's gaze met mine. "It's hope. A future I think we all need and want."

"Exactly," Cheshire chimed in, the corner of his mouth twitching upward. "A place where our kids can ride bikes and play hide-and-seek. Where we watch each other's backs by just looking out the window."

"Where we grow old, but never alone," Absolem concluded, pushing his glasses higher on his nose with a rare, content smile.

Their dream would bind us tighter as a family. This wasn't just about having a house. These men were building a legacy one home at a time. A place where they could grow old together with their families, and one day our children would take over. It was beautiful, and I was so happy to be a part of it.

Jo took my hand and guided me to the kitchen, where I found March leaning over some papers strewn across the kitchen table. Rabbit and Tweedle were flanking him. I took a peek and saw what appeared to be a map of the future of this place. Houses marked off as little rectangles, a square marked *playground*, and I noticed other things like a pool and pavilion.

"See here?" Absolem's finger traced along a section of the plans, his blue eyes serious behind the lenses. "We can extend this part out. More space if we need it in the future, although I think Hatter is set on the club staying the size it is."

"Good thinking," March rumbled, his voice low like distant thunder.

In this place our children would never know the fears that haunted our pasts, not if we could help it. The Underland MC wasn't just a club. These men were building a sanctuary.

"Thank you," I whispered, gratitude swelling in my chest. "For everything. For welcoming me into your family, not turning me away when I showed up uninvited, and for giving all of us something we so badly need."

"Family looks out for each other, Violet," March said, echoing my thoughts, his blue eyes locking with mine. "Always."

In his eyes I saw it clear as day -- hope. It glowed bright, and in that look, we shared it all -- the dreams of kids playing in a yard we could defend, the laughter that would echo off our homes filled with love and not fear. I didn't know the background of everyone here. But I knew their time in the military had changed them all in different ways. They needed this as much as Jo, Eliza, and I did.

"I don't know about Jo and Violet, but Eliza likes plants. Maybe we could have a community garden," Cheshire chimed in, his usually mischievous face serious. "One for vegetables and fruit too. Teach the kids to grow their own, you know? Maybe tending to plants would be calming for some of us."

I noticed the way his gaze shot over to Rabbit, who even now seemed a little jittery.

"Self-sufficiency," I said. "Well, somewhat anyway. We'd obviously still need other stuff from town, but it would cut costs on some of the groceries, depending on how large of a space we're talking about."

"Exactly." March nodded.

"Renewable energy sources." Absolem's brow furrowed and he folded his arms over his chest. "Maybe we could put in solar panels for the houses. Clubhouse too. It would not only cut costs but would be beneficial to the planet as well."

I had to press my lips together to keep from laughing. It was hard to imagine the tough biker being concerned about going green. But I liked it.

"What about adding security systems to the houses?" Eliza asked. "Even if this place would be mostly safe, someone managed to snatch Violet right from under our noses. It would be nice to have an extra layer of safety when we're home."

"Right." March scanned the papers in front of him. "We need to do something about our perimeter too. Houses first, obviously, but I think we should work on completely fencing this place in like the Reckless Kings did."

Absolem cleared his throat. "I could install cameras throughout, even though it wouldn't necessarily keep something from happening, it would let us see what transpired. If we'd been able to see someone take Violet, we could have gotten to her faster."

"All good points. We have some time. It will be probably a month before we can even bring in the first house. Maybe longer," Hatter said.

Everyone continued to bounce ideas around, and I could feel the excitement in the air. We were planning for a future where violence and chaos were kept at bay by the walls we'd build and the bonds we shared. I couldn't wait to see how it all turned out, and I was excited to help wherever I could.

"Architects of a better tomorrow," Jo said. "This place is going to be amazing!"

"What do we do with all the rooms in the clubhouse if everyone is moving out?" Eliza asked.

"Well, we could combine two of them into a space for club meetings," Cheshire said.

"Church. It's called Church," March said. "And I agree we definitely need to do that. We'd have to take out at least one of the bathrooms to pull it off, but I don't think that will be an issue. Just need to hire a plumber so we don't end up flooding this place."

"That still leaves a lot of space," I said. "What about turning one of the rooms into a community pantry for cans and dry goods? We could stockpile non-perishables so that if anything happens, we're somewhat prepared."

"Like another pandemic," Jo said. "Or worse… if someone is after the club, we could hole up behind the fence and be fine for a while."

I noticed Absolem was making notes. It looked like the club was going to consider all our ideas. I liked how the men weren't excluding us and letting the women have input. This was our home too, after all.

March stood beside me, his hand warm on my back. He leaned in, nodding toward the men who had become our brothers in more than just name. "These men are my brothers, which means they're yours as well, Violet. Our kid is going to have two aunts and lots of uncles. You're no longer alone."

"Family," Hatter said. "We're all one big family. Always will be."

"This isn't a place that will ever tear you down," Absolem said. "We all build each other up, support one another, and there are lots of shoulders to lean on if you ever need one."

"Thank you," I said again, feeling the words were too small, too simple for the gratitude swelling inside me.

"None of that now," Hatter's voice cut through the thick air, commanding yet kind. "There's no need for thanks."

"Here's to the future," March raised an invisible glass, his lips quirking in a half-smile that reached his eyes.

"To the future," we all echoed.

Soon, the room began to empty, the energy shifting as the club members stepped out. The murmurs of conversation drifted back into the clubhouse, threads weaving together, stitching us tighter. Something inside me loosened, and I realized how comfortable I felt here.

I followed March out, the last to leave. I thought about the nursery the club had prepared. It wasn't just a room. It was a promise. Our children would know laughter here, not fear. They'd know love, surrounded by the roar of engines and the fierce hearts of the Underland MC. Our little community wouldn't just be buildings. It was so much more.

Chapter Nineteen
March

We rode in silence, with my large frame crammed into Violet's little car. Now that she was a little over six months pregnant, I didn't want to risk her riding on my bike. I was both excited and apprehensive about this visit with the doctor. We were finally going to find out if we were having a girl or a boy.

Pulling into the parking lot, I killed the engine and helped Violet out of the car. She unfolded herself from the seat, her movements careful, protective of the life she carried. Her eyes flickered with a mix of fear and anticipation, the shadows of her past lingering just beneath the surface.

"Ready for this?" I asked.

She nodded, biting her lip. "As I'll ever be."

We stepped through the sliding doors, the sterile scent of antiseptic filling my nostrils.

"Mr. and Mrs. Blevins?" The nurse's voice cut through my thoughts like a knife.

"Right here," I said, squeezing Violet's hand. It wasn't often I got to hear Violet called by her married name. *My* name. I had to admit I rather liked it.

The doctor's examination room felt too small, the walls closing in as we took our seats. The crinkle of the paper cover on the exam table sounded much too loud. Violet's hand felt small and warm in mine.

"Deep breaths. We've got this." I kept my tone even, controlled, despite the adrenaline coursing through my veins.

She offered me a frail smile, her strength shining through despite the quiver in her lips. "I know. Just... can't help but worry, you know? What if something doesn't look right?"

"Hey, I'm right here with you. Whatever comes, we face it head-on. Together." I gave her hand a reassuring squeeze, and she leaned into me, her body melding against mine.

"Thank you," she whispered.

This was our second attempt to find out if we were having a girl or boy. Last time, the machine hadn't been working so we'd had to reschedule. The doctor came in, greeted us, then got down to business. A technician rolled the ultrasound machine closer and lifted Violet's shirt over her stomach. She smeared gel across Violet's belly, and I felt her tense up beside me. My gaze locked onto the screen, every muscle coiled tight, ready for whatever was coming. The doctor had said everything seemed to be fine at the last appointment, but I couldn't help but worry.

"Okay, let's see what we've got here," the doctor murmured, watching the technician move the transducer in slow circles. Images flickered, shades of gray and black dancing before us. Rorschach blots as far as I was concerned. Ones that held our future.

Violet's gaze met mine, her eyes wide and searching. I knew this visit had been worrying her. I didn't understand why, but as her anxiety had just spiked, so had mine.

"Shh, I'm here." I squeezed her hand, trying to calm her down.

"Ah, there we go," the doctor announced, a note of triumph in her voice as if they'd uncovered hidden treasure. Which in a way, they had. The image on the screen sharpened, and my heart hammered against my ribcage. The doctor measured our baby before the technician moved the wand around a bit more.

"Congratulations, it's a girl!" The words cut

through the tension like a knife through leather.

A girl. *Our* girl.

Shit. Was I prepared to have a daughter? If she met a man like me, I would probably lose my shit. I hadn't exactly been a saint before falling in love with Violet. Maybe not as much of a hound as some men I knew, but still.

Vi's hand gripped mine. Pure joy mingled with an edge of disbelief, as if fate had finally dealt us a winning hand. Our daughter seemed to be perfect from what I could tell looking at the screen. But it didn't hurt to be certain.

"A little girl," I murmured. "And she's healthy? No noticeable defects or anything?"

The doctor nodded. "Yep. Everything looks good."

We finished the rest of the visit quickly and stopped at the front desk to schedule the next one before going back out to the car. My arm snaked around Vi's waist, pulling her into me with a force that bordered on desperation. Emotions churned inside like a tempest -- relief, awe, love -- all crashing together.

"A little girl... Benni," she murmured. "Let's name her Benni, after Ben. Is that okay?"

Ben. My brother-in-arms, the ghost who had never truly left us. I could only imagine how much he would love knowing his niece carried his name.

"That's perfect," I managed to say, my voice gruff from the emotions churning inside me. Benni. Our little girl would know of her uncle, the hero, the lost soul we clung to even as we forged ahead. Violet and I would both share stories about him, and I'd make damn sure our new home had a picture of him. We had quite a few.

Benni. Our daughter. Our hope.

"I think Benni is an excellent name, and I bet her uncle would be thrilled. We'll make sure she knows all about him," I said.

Violet nodded. The air between us crackled with an electric charge, the future unfurling like a road laid out before us, untraveled and beckoning. Neither of us had ever considered marriage and a baby. Not really. When she was younger, she may have pictured me as her groom, but as she'd gotten older those dreams had faded thanks to reality. Life could be hard and cruel. It had a way of crushing you. Yet here we were. I couldn't speak for Violet, but I was eager for this next adventure. I didn't know shit about babies, but I'd learn. I wanted to be a good dad to little Benni.

Violet's hand, still clasped in mine, was a lifeline -- a tangible reminder of the life we were weaving together.

"I can't believe we're having a little girl." She looked up at me. "It seems more real today than ever before, now that she has a name."

My chest swelled, heart hammering against my ribcage as if trying to match the cadence of our unborn daughter's tiny heartbeat. "I can and I will protect her, love her, and make sure she has the best life possible."

"I know." Violet leaned her head against my shoulder. "You're going to be an amazing dad. I can already tell. I have a feeling our Benni is going to be a daddy's girl."

I kissed her temple. "Then we'll need to have a little boy who adores his mom just as much and can grow up big and strong to help protect his sister."

She nudged me with her elbow. "Or you can teach her to protect herself. Why should she need a man to do the job for her?"

I paused. Good idea. "I like that. She doesn't

need any man in her life except me and her uncles. I'll teach her how to fix a car, ride a motorcycle, shoot a gun, and put a man on his ass if he does something he shouldn't."

Violet rolled her eyes. "Of course, you will."

I leaned down to kiss her before helping her into the car. The ride back to the clubhouse was quiet. The doctor had given Violet a picture of little Benni and she kept staring at it. I would have too if I hadn't been the one driving. I couldn't wait to show everyone our daughter.

When we got back to the clubhouse, I walked in ahead of Vi, and immediately grabbed everyone's attention.

"We have something to share!" My voice boomed through the space and made everyone stop and face me. They eyed Violet beside me, or more accurately the little piece of paper in her hand.

"It's a girl," she said. "We're naming her Benni, after my brother."

A collective breath, held in suspense, broke free in cheers and claps, the sound ricocheting off the walls. I could tell my brothers, those who had also known Ben, were thrilled with her name choice. We all missed him, and now he would not only live on in our memories, but also through our child.

Eliza, her belly now just as big as Violet's, sidled up beside my wife, a smile gracing her lips. "Can't wait to meet little Benni."

Jo shuffled closer, her own stomach just as large, as all three women were due within weeks of each other. There was a spark in her eyes as she hugged Violet.

"Three little ones on the way," she said. "I'm not sure all these big tough bikers can handle three crying babies at once. Might be fun to watch."

"Seems like Underland's future is set on growing," I stated, the corner of my mouth lifting in a half-grin. "It won't be long before the next generation is here."

Eliza's hand hovered over her stomach, her eyes alight with a secret she was about to spill. Up until now, both she and Jo had remained silent as to whether they were having boys or girls. I wondered if we were about to find out.

"Guess what?" Her voice was steady, strong. "It's a boy. We haven't decided on a name yet, though."

"Me too," Jo said. "Another boy."

The club clapped and whistled at the news, everyone excited about the new little ones joining us soon.

Then Absolem leaned in, a smirk playing on his lips. Something told me I wasn't going to like whatever came out of his mouth.

"Well, Violet, looks like your little girl might have her pick of the boys in the future." His words were teasing, and yet I wanted to punch him for it.

Violet's laughter danced in the air. "I'm not sure she could handle either of them, and her daddy has already decided she'll never need a man except him and her uncles."

"Damn straight! You better train those two to think of Benni as their cousin or sister. Anything other than a marriage option."

Jo snickered. "Like I want a daughter-in-law who might take after you, March. I bet your little one is going to be a hellion."

I nodded. "I'm okay with that."

"Don't jinx my son with that bullshit," Hatter

called out. "I want him to find some sweet, quiet girl."

"Wouldn't dream of it, Prez," Absolem said, a hand over his heart as if pledging an oath.

The room erupted then, laughter bouncing off the walls. It was a good sound, a free sound. The club members were a rough bunch, scars and ink etched into their skin like the stories of their lives, but in this moment, they were just family. A family about to welcome new life into its fold.

"All right, all right," Mock piped up. "Let's not get ahead of ourselves. They aren't even born yet."

"True," I conceded, throwing an arm around Violet's shoulders. "But it's never too early to start worrying as a father, right?"

"You got that right," someone from the back called, and more chuckles threaded through the air.

My gaze slid over to Violet, her eyes bright. She was strength personified, the woman who'd stand by my side through the storms ahead. And we'd weather them together.

"Here's to Benni," I raised my voice, lifting a beer Cheshire passed to me, "and to the next generation of Underland. May they ride harder, live braver, and love stronger than we ever did."

"Here, here!" The chorus came loud and unified, glasses lifted high.

And just like that, our little girl was toasted by the toughest, most loyal band of misfits I had ever known.

The room quieted down, and everyone went back to what they'd been doing before we arrived. I scanned the faces around us. Men who were still fighting their demons but had hope for a brighter future. I tightened my hold on Violet, thankful to have her here by my side.

"Never thought I'd see the day," I murmured, meeting her gaze. I placed my hand over her belly. "Our own little warrior."

"Warrior? I suppose. After all, she'll be just like her daddy."

I shook my head, my heart swelling. "Nah, she'll be better. She's got you in her corner."

Violet leaned into me, her forehead resting against my shoulder. A moment of peace in a life too often marked by chaos. The club, it was our sanctuary, our battlefield, and now, it was going to be Benni's home.

"Family," she whispered. "You've given me that and so much more, March. Coming to find you was the best thing I ever did."

"Damn right." I looked around at the patched vests and lined faces. These men and women, they weren't just comrades. They were the guardians of our future. Not just ours, but the entire town of Warren. We'd made this place our home, and we'd defend it with everything we had.

"Let's make a promise," I said, my voice steady as I spoke to all three women, as well as Hatter and Cheshire. "We keep the roads safe for our kids. We give them the freedom we never had. And we won't hold them back from chasing their dreams, even if it takes them far from home."

"Promise," they echoed back.

Our Underland MC family, bound not just by blood or ink but by the hope of what lay ahead. With every rev of an engine, every clink of metal, and every cry of new life joining us, we were forging a new path -- one where Benni, Eliza's boy, and Jo's boy would have better lives than any of us had ever dreamed of.

"Here's to tomorrow," I declared, raising my

beer.

"To tomorrow," they answered.

And as I held Violet close, feeling the thrum of life within her, I knew there was nothing we wouldn't face to protect this dream. Nothing we wouldn't conquer. Because we were Underland -- unbreakable, united, unstoppable.

I couldn't wait to see what the future had in store for us next…

Epilogue
March
Two Months Later

With Violet due within a few months, I'd been doing my best to make this place as secure as possible. Absolem had found the perfect cameras for the clubhouse and had ordered extras for all our homes. Even the ones not installed yet. Buying prefab homes had made things go quickly once the land had been cleared and pipes and wires had been run to each homesite.

The fact we'd paid extra to have it done quickly hadn't hurt either. As of now, three of us had homes, and Rabbit would have one by end of next week. I'd had cameras placed over both exterior doors to the clubhouse, two on either side of the building, making sure the entire side was in view of at least one camera, and I'd done the same to the homes already set up.

Absolem had access to the feed from his computer, as did Hatter, Cheshire, and myself. We could even view the feeds from our phones if we wanted. I'd gone an extra step and put an alarm system in my place, and I knew Hatter and Cheshire were planning to do the same. The three of us were neighbors, with Hatter in the center. It worked out well since the ladies enjoyed spending so much time together.

I stood in the living room, watching them from the window. It was still too chilly to plant flowers, but we'd cleared a space for a garden, and Hatter had already gifted them with a table and chairs. The flowers would form a ring around the area with cobblestones under the table once spring arrived.

The three of them looked happy these days. Hell,

I was happier than I'd ever been. I left my spot by the window and went into the nursery I'd set up last week. We'd decided to keep the walls a neutral color, and Violet had accented the space with pictures. She'd talked me into pink and purple for our girl, even though the room felt far too dainty for someone like me to dare step foot inside it.

We'd already picked out some toys and books. I'd even put a bookshelf and toy chest together, as well as a crib, changing table, and rocking chair. The room wasn't huge, and I'd convinced Vi to stop adding more large items. When she insisted the baby needed a dresser, I found a small four-drawer chest and tucked it into the closet. As tiny as our daughter would be the first few years, anything that needed to hang on the rack still wouldn't brush the top of the chest. It was the best solution I could come up with.

I went to the kitchen and grabbed a beer from the fridge before taking a seat. Not for the first time, I wondered what life would be like right now if Ben had survived. Even if Vi and I had ended up together, would he be happy for us? Would we be sharing a drink right this very moment? Or would he be worried I'd break his sister's heart?

I lifted my bottle. "Here's to you, Ben. Wish you were still with us. Miss you like hell, and I know Vi does too."

I heard a throat clear and glanced at the back door. Shit. I hadn't even heard the fucker come in. "I may not be Ben, but can I join you?"

"Sure, Tweedle. Beer's in the fridge. Help yourself."

He did just that before sitting in the spot across from me. He eyed me, as if weighing his words and deciding what he should and shouldn't say.

"When are you going to stop living in the past?" he asked. "You have a wife, a home, a baby on the way. Ben wouldn't want you to dwell on what happened to him or sit here pondering all the what-ifs. I may not have met him, but I can tell that much from the way everyone talks about him."

I nodded. "Yeah, guess so. Sometimes it's just hard. Every memory I have of Vi, before she showed up here, has Ben in it. She was always chasing after us, wanting to do whatever we were doing. I always thought she just adored her big brother. Never occurred to me she had a crush on me."

"Look at all the time you wasted." Tweedle smirked. "If you hadn't been running away, you may have married Violet a lot sooner. Been happier for it too, I'm sure."

"Possibly. Not sure I was ready for all this back then. Hell, sometimes I'm not sure I'm ready now."

"You are." Tweedle took a swallow of his beer. "Anyone can see it. The two of you were meant to be together, and I have to agree with what Vi has said several times. You're going to be a great dad. Probably overprotective, though."

I shrugged. "Can you blame me? I'm having a daughter. Scares the shit out of me. What if some asshole comes along and takes advantage of her? Or lures her in with sweet words and she runs off with him?"

"Then we track him down, break his balls, and bring her home." He pointed the neck of his bottle toward me. "That little one is my niece. You think I'm letting anyone run off with her? Hell no. Same goes for the rest of us."

"Yeah. You're right. She'll have lots of protection around here. As long as Hatter's and Cheshire's sons think of her as a sister, we're good. If either of them even thinks of dating her, the Pres and VP may have to file missing persons reports on their boys."

Tweedle snickered. "I can see that. Understand it too."

"Any news on the fence line?" I asked.

"Absolem is picky as fuck about it. Think he's shelling out the cash for something custom. Too big to climb over. Solid so it can't be cut with wire cutters. And he wants cameras installed there too. He said he's not taking any more chances."

Good. It's what we needed to do. What should have been done already. Since he'd been snatching the funds from known traffickers, rapists, and drug cartels, I didn't care about the cost. Neither did anyone else here. At least all that dirty money was being put to good use, and anytime he found a paper trail for a woman being enslaved in this country, he sent an anonymous tip to the Feds. No clue what the hell he did with the ones overseas.

One day at a time, we were doing our best to make not only this town but this world a better place. It's why we'd all joined the military to begin with. We wanted to make a difference. Not sure I accomplished that as a Marine, but I knew things were changing now. At the very least, in Warren things were different. The interim sheriff was now the full-fledged one. The town had voted him into office, and it had been a landslide. I almost felt sorry for the poor asshole who ran against him.

"What do you think about the club's plans for the future?" Tweedle asked.

"You already know I'm all for it. Why? Think we're getting too domesticated or something?"

"Not exactly. I never wanted to be party central.

I've heard a lot of clubs have a wild time. It's fine every now and then, but… after the shit we've been through, I like the quiet."

I got it. We all did. It's a large part of why we'd decided not to open anything like a bar or strip club. Instead, the ladies had talked us into two businesses. An auto repair shop that also worked on motorcycles, and guards for short-time hire. We'd accept contracts for up to a month, anywhere in the country, as long as the client paid for travel and accommodations as part of the fee. I'd opted to work in the shop twice a week. We were all taking turns, but I didn't want to travel far for any reason right now. I wanted to be here for Vi and our baby.

"Aren't you leaving soon?" I asked.

He nodded. "Yep. Some little princess needs a guard for a few days down in Florida. I have to admit, I wouldn't mind some warmer weather. Maybe I can hit the beach when I'm not on duty."

"Good luck. Better you than me."

Tweedle finished his beer and stood up, tossing it into the trash. "Well, I'm out. But seriously, March. Don't sit here and brood. Go enjoy the fresh air, spend time with your woman, or go for a fucking ride. Sitting at your kitchen table thinking about Ben is pathetic. Even he would say so."

I flipped him off, and he laughed as he let himself out the back door. He made a good point though. My woman didn't need me right now, so… that left going for a ride. I grabbed my keys and stepped out the front door. Walking over to the ladies, I leaned down and kissed Vi's cheek.

"Where are you off to?" she asked.

"Ride. I'll be back within an hour. Maybe less. You call if you need me. I'll have the phone on vibrate so I'll know to pull over."

"Have fun." She gave me a little wave, and I took that as my cue to leave.

I got on my bike, started her up, and headed for the gates. For now, they remained open, but one day they wouldn't. My bike ate up the miles on the road as I headed down the two-lane highway out of town, taking the winding road through the mountains. With the wind in my hair, the sun on my face, and a lighter heart than I'd had in a while, I couldn't help but smile.

This… This was what life was all about.

Harley Wylde

Harley Wylde is an accomplished author known for her captivating MC Romances. With an unwavering commitment to sensual storytelling, Wylde immerses her readers in an exciting world of fierce men and irresistible women. Her works exude passion, danger, and gritty realism, while still managing to end on a satisfying note each time.

When not crafting her tales, Wylde spends her time brainstorming new plotlines, indulging in a hot cup of Starbucks, or delving into a good book. She has a particular affinity for supernatural horror literature and movies. Visit Wylde's website to learn more about her works and upcoming events, and don't forget to sign up for her newsletter to receive exclusive discounts and other exciting perks.

Harley at Changeling: changelingpress.com/harley-wylde-a-196

Bad Boys Multiverse

Contemporary MC, Organized Crime, and Crossovers
- A Bad Boy Romance
- Dixie Reapers MC
- Devil's Boneyard MC
- Hades Abyss MC
- Devil's Fury MC
- Reckless Kings MC
- Savage Raptors MC
- Swift Angels MC
- Owned by the Mob
- Bryson Corners
- Underland MC

Paranormal MC
- Devoted Guardians MC
- Balor's Saints MC

Print and Audio:
- Dixie Reapers MC Print
- Dixie Reapers MC Audio
- Devil's Boneyard MC Audio
- Hades Abyss MC Audio
- Devil's Fury MC Audio

Changeling Press LLC

Contemporary Action Adventure, Sci-Fi, Steampunk, Dark Fantasy, Urban Fantasy, Paranormal, and BDSM Romance available in e-book, audio, and print format at ChangelingPress.com -- MC Romance, Werewolves, Vampires, Dragons, Shapeshifters and Horror -- Tales from the edge of your imagination.

Where can I get Changeling Press Books?

Changeling Press e-books are available at ChangelingPress.com, Amazon, Apple Books, Barnes & Noble, Kobo, Smashwords, and other online retailers, including Everand and Kobo Subscription Services. Print books are available at Amazon, Barnes and Noble, and by ISBN special order through your local bookstores.

ChangelingPress.com

Made in the USA
Middletown, DE
17 September 2025